THE HIDDEN SIN

BY

R.J. LEVESQUE

The Hidden Sin Volume 1:
Lies & Confessions

© 2010 R.J. Levesque (Lulu Author)

ISBN: 978-0-9867191-0-3

Published by Rikky J. Levesque

Printed by Lulu Press Inc.
ID# 9262348

www.lulu.com

For my Mom, Dad, Sister
and rest of Family
and
Friends

Prologue

"I can't believe you!" Carol shouted. "You are actually gonna do that?"

"I'm sorry, Carol." Karen replied with tears in her eyes. "But I feel that it is the right thing to do."

"After all these years, I helped you getting to this point in your school life and now your gonna throw it all away because your conscious tells you?"

"I've already written the speech. I will tell everyone the truth and I don't care if I have to redo school all over again."

Carol looked into Karen's eyes and let out a big sigh. She slowly shook her head and looked away with disappointment. She could not believe that she would be betrayed by her longtime and childhood friend. She had helped her several times throughout her life and when Karen had told her about what was she gonna do at their graduation, she felt like receiving a huge slap in the face.

"I'm sorry, Carol." Karen repeated under more tears.

Her friend raised a finger. "Don't, Karen. If you're gonna go down, I'm not going down with you. Consider that as my final word."

Karen said nothing. She already felt the bond that those girls had was severed the minute she told Carol the plan. And it was finally confirmed when little friendship ring that Karen had given her had been taken off and thrown right at her face, bounced off her left cheek.

"And consider that as you and I are no longer friends." Carol spoke sneeringly. "Now, get out of my house and out of my sight."

Karen slowly turned toward the front door and slowly opened it. She only stood in the doorway for about a few seconds hoping to get another glance at her former friend, but Carol was too angry and Karen did not want to see that expression again since she already saw it before. And without saying goodbye, nor a sign of departure, Karen had exited Carol's house and into the evening streets.

Karen started walking, heading toward home. But along the way, another one of her friends was already in view by the street lamps that illuminated the darkened roads. The smile on that person's face and the light wave had already given Karen the clue that it was Alice Craig.

"Hey, Karen." she said as she was able to get closer.

"Hi, Alice." Karen spoke softly, wiping the tears and tried to hide the crying.

Alice noticed that Karen was upset about something. She didn't asked why nor that she wanted to, but she was happy enough to see her classmate out in the streets at night.

"Did you came from Carol's?" Alice asked.

"Yeah," Karen replied. "I just told her that I've finished the valedictory speech."

"That's good. I can't wait to hear it at the graduation. I have a funny feeling that it's gonna be a good one."

Karen slightly nodded. "Yeah, it will be something to think about."

"Well, I'm heading to the church to see Pastor Mayne. I'll see you tomorrow. Goodnight, Karen."

Alice walked away and disappeared into the darkness as Karen continued walking home.

Karen arrived home and spotted her mother and father in the living room watching TV. The mother was busy knitting a blanket for a friend she knew at the nearby supermarket and she was the first person who heard the front door opening and closing. But her father was too interested in watching a stand-up comedy program, he couldn't care less about who walked into the house. His eyes were glued to the screen and had laughed to whatever joke the stand-up comedian threw at him.

"Hey, honey." her mother said. "How's your time with Carol?"

Karen did not want to talk about it because of the fight her and her former friend had.

"It was fine." she said as she kept on walking toward the staircase that lead straight to the her room, trying to avoid any further conversations with her mother.

"Is something wrong?" her mother asked as she noticed her daughter's expression was showing that she was upset and had cried recently.

"No, I'm alright." Karen quickly responded. "I'm going to bed."

"Okay. Night, dear."

Karen arrived in her bedroom and closed the door fast. She then sat in front of her desk for a minute and her head had finally landed on her folded arms which were quickly lifted onto the desk and bawled her tears away. She knew this would be hard on her, and to tell her friend, who she had quickly severed their friendship, it was worse. After all the years she had been in school, all the effort she had put in, and she was gonna throw it all away. It was the right thing to do.

Before she was well enough to go directly to bed, she took out her pink-coloured diary and began to write down her newest entry. Even writing it was hard for her, since she recently lost her best friend. But her diary was her only salvation to let her true feelings come alive. Her secrets, her desires and her passion were written across several pages, several dates and several months. But the one she wrote under heavy sadness took her longer than ones that she had written before.

Back downstairs, Karen's mother was a little concerned about her daughter nearly rushing up the stairs and into her bedroom. But since it was already getting late, she thought it would be best to let her be until the next morning. She had put away her knitting needles and was about to get off from her rocking chair until she heard a loud tumbling noise from directly above, where Karen's bedroom was. The sound had nearly made his father jumped and nearly snapped out of the trance he was on from watching the television.

Both of her parents went upstairs to see if their daughter was alright but when they got to her bedroom, she was nowhere to be seen. The chair in which she sat had fallen backwards and right in front of their feet, was a large, black body print that shaped and resembled like their daughter.

The father checked the window outside and the mother checked under the bed, Karen was no where to be found. They went back downstairs and out of the house to see if she had gone out but there was no one there except one person who appeared to be an old man who had fallen off a tall tree standing nearby with its branches reaching out toward the left side of the house.

With their daughter vanished, and with no trace of her in sight and a black print was left in her wake, they had no choice but to call the police.

VOLUME 1

LIES & CONFESSIONS

Chapter 1

Nobody likes to be woken up by the sound of an alarm clock, not even Jake Miller himself. The buzzing, piercing, monotonous sound that resembled a broken mechanical rooster, was ramming through his ears and disturbed his sleep. If he cannot silence the annoying sound, he would go mad and it would stay in his brain most of his teenage life. Luckily, his alarm clock had a reset button so that it would go off the next day. He would rather press that instead of the snooze button because that would only pause the alarm for about ten minutes and it would mock at him again. And that is what he did, he pressed the reset button and fell back asleep. Of course, he would fall back if his Aunt Laura had not walked into his bedroom.

"Rise and shine, Jake!" Aunt Laura said with a smile.

Jake groaned and tried to shoo her aunt away.

"What you talking about?"

"Today's the big day." Laura tried to shaking him. "Graduation day!"

Those two words had made Jake's eyes widened. His aunt was right, it was the day of his graduation from Greensburg High School. After twelve years of studies from the alphabet to calculus, after twelves years of doing 'Simon Says' and solving math problems using letters and fractions, the day had finally come for him claim his reward for all the hard work and digesting headache pills. That day, he would get his diploma, walk out of the front entrance of the school and go further in his studies.

That wasn't really his plan, though. Jake had no idea what to do with his life after he had done school. When you were a child, you had dreams. Dreams of becoming a doctor, a firefighter, a teacher, any of those professions. But when you grow up, you realize that you have to work at it to become one of those. You can't become a doctor or a teacher just by wishing it. You have to do what your parents had done, which is going to school, get an education and get some training in the field you had wished for since childhood. So to put it in simpler terms, your dream job gets shattered by the harsh concept known as reality. You must work your ass off toward your goal and proving to the people who had already reached that goal that you can be with them or surpass them.

Jake had a dream to become a cop, a detective just like his father. But unfortunately, his dream of becoming one had disappeared since his father was shot and killed on duty, at a convenient store in Carlton City, located about four hundred kilometres North of Greensburg. He an his mother had moved to Greensburg when he was only six, due to the fact that his father was so dedicated to his job and felt by staying at Carlton City would help clean it up. His mother did not want her family to be raised in a city full of crime and corruption but wanted a quiet, peaceful life, a place where Jake can feel comfortable and not being afraid. So, without divorcing, Jake's father had promised to visit them every month on a weekend to spend some quality time with his family. But there was one month that he never showed up, and that was when they heard the bad news.

Jake had finally got out of bed and went to the bathroom for a morning shower. After he was finished, he looked himself in the mirror. He saw the reflection of a lazy-looking sixteen-year-old schmuck with his short, chestnut hair soaked in hot water. He stared into the his hazel eyes with a smirk on his face.

"Way to go, you lucky bastard." he said to his mirrored twin.

After he dried himself and got changed, his aunt called out from underneath him for breakfast. After a short trip down the stairs he saw a foot-long stack of pancakes sitting on the centre of the dining table. He also realized that he won't be having breakfast alone since his nine-year-old cousin Becky was already sitting at the right side of the table, eating cereal and reading her comics without a single care in the world.

The usual pony-tailed, freckled-faced, tooth-missing child was a bit of a handful but she had always managed to cheer her big cousin up when ever Jake felt down. Because not only he lost a good father, he also lost his mother. She had committed suicide upon great depression which began with his father's death. He couldn't remember much but it happened one month after his father's funeral, and remembered what he

14

saw that night. The six-year-old Jake was about to go to the bathroom when he heard a faint noise, a faint creaking noise like an old rocking chair. And just like every curious little boy, he went to see where that noise was coming from.

The upstairs hallway was dark by the night sky with only a little light coming through the window at the end, beaming from a nearby street light. The hallway had stretched down and made a sharp, left turn to where his mother's bedroom would be found. Following the creaking noise, he slowly walked toward the sound down the hallway but feeling a bit scared. Every child in his age had always been afraid of things that go bump in the night, like the bogeyman or monsters in their closets or gremlins under their beds. And just like every child in his age, he was hoping none of those things would appear out from the darkness as he traverse further down the hallway. As soon as he reached the end toward window, he slowly turned left to where the path had stopped. In front of him was a door that was slightly opened inward and a little light from what he assumed it was a night lamp next to her mother's bed.

The creaking noise was louder and Jake reached out his little fingers, gently pushing the door. When it finally opened wide enough for Jake to see in, he saw where the creaking noise was coming from. Up on the ceiling was a small lamp with a dirty, old rope tied to it, making the creaking noise due to a slow, swinging motion and by whatever weight it was being held on. Jake's eyes followed the rope downward to which it formed several horizontal loops and the last loop was found around a pink-skinned neck. It was wrapped around it so tight that even veins were shown popping out, trying to get the blood through. Then he saw the entire image, and froze with shock. His mother's face was shown with her cold blue eyes staring into nothingness with no smile, no laughter, no life at all. There were tears on her face that signified that she had cried before she became what her son had seen. She was an empty shell, a shadow of her former self. Jake had even called out to her but there was no answer, not a single voice, not a single breath. It was as if she had disappeared from the face of the earth and left this empty shell hanging by the neck.

Jake was so in shock the he could not remember anything that happened before that. His doctor said he had suffered some sort of memory loss due to what happened and even during his graduation he still couldn't remember the time between her suicide and the last time she smiled at him. All he had known is that after his mother's funeral, her sister Laura decided that he should live with her for the time being.

She was so close to her sister that she couldn't believe that a kind and gentle woman had decided to take her own life and there was no suicide note not even a written letter to her loved ones. Laura had thought that she had gone so deep in her depression that even writing a note would be painful. Jake had missed his mother so much that every night he would stare at the photo of the two of them and shed a tear.

Greensburg High School was flooded with families gathering together anxiously for the ceremony. Some of them were still standing outside while the rest were in the school's gymnasium, waiting patiently and talking to each other. Many of them had their digital cameras and picture phones in handy for when the time their child received their diploma, they would take a snap shot to capture the moment. Families, relatives, and friends were glowing with proud faces, except for one family. The married couple were smiling but they had also shown signs of sadness, as if they had lost their child but also have hope in their hearts for that child's safe return.

About one week before Graduation Day, one of the Greensburg High School graduates, who was also a valedictorian, was reported missing. The seventeen-year-old girl's goal in life was to become a psychiatrist and had received full recommendation from her chemistry teacher, Dr. William Cummings. He was suffering from an emotional breakdown since his wife was killed in a freeway accident and had shown potential signs of suicide. He wasn't so sure if he wanted to continue on with his life while suffering this terrible loss. He would just kill himself just to see her again, but Karen Hannah had convinced him that taking his own life just to see her wife again is not the way. His wife wouldn't even want that from him and even if he did, he would probably suffer even more in the afterlife. Karen told him that if he kept her wife so close to her heart and kept memories of her alive, then she would be standing next to him smiling. She would wanted him to move on and live happily with her in spirit and they will eventually be together again. The entire session had made tears in the doctor 's eyes and personally went to the principal of the school to recommend Karen full scholarship for her future studies in psychiatry. Though it was sad to think that she may have missed the opportunity.

Karen had been missing for several days and without no clue where she had gone and her parents had been waiting patiently for her safe return. When the police arrived at their house they searched her bedroom for anything that might give a clue to where she had gone, like a letter, note or even photograph. But what they found in her upstairs bedroom was a bit peculiar. On the floor behind a tipped over chair near her desk was a huge black stain on the wooden floor. The stain somehow shaped in a peculiar way that resembled a silhouette of a person, a possible silhouette of Karen. The stain was deep into the wood itself like it was either burned or painted on. This had made the police confused but with all confusion aside, they decided to locate her by any means. But after a week of searching and asking questions around the town, there was no lead, no hint to where she may have gone.

Jake was in his homeroom classroom as well as all of his graduating classmates. After glancing at them for a few minutes, he was thinking of the friends he had made through out his school life and how this memorable day where they all get their diplomas, go on their separate ways and fulfill their ultimate dream. But he was sure that he would cross paths with them sometime in the near future. There was one classmate that he admired most was Alice Craig, aiming to become a fashion designer. Her gentle face and kind smile reminded him of his mother when she last smiled at him. Her brunette hair was fine and natural looking, all the way down between her shoulder blades and her blue eyes were bright and calm. Her voice was soft as if the heavens have given her the voice of an angel. Whenever she spoke, it was like Jake's worries and anxieties had been washed away and made him smile even for short while. But even a girl as beautiful and talented as her, Jake had no chance of having her since she was dating Jason Baker.

Back in Junior High, Jason Baker was the usual bully. Always pushing people around, gotten away with trouble, looking down on others. He was always a real bully to Jake, always claiming that he was gonna steal Alice away from him by making threats. Even when Alice approached Jake just by friendly means, he made stupid claims that he was seducing her. Jason was a real sports jockey, though he could not seem to stay in one sport. At first he wanted to do baseball. Then as years went by he wanted to do basketball. But then, closing in on his graduation, he changed his mind again and decided he wanted to do football mainly because he was a tough guy and liked pushing, shoving and tackling people all over the place. Luckily for him, after graduation, he would go up North to Carlton City and to meet the coach for city's team for try-outs. With his ginger-coloured hair, pudgy face and medium build, he would resemble a cartoon character who happened to be a sports nut equipped with an empty, one-tracked mind.

Then there was Carol Graham, another bright student in Jake's graduating class. Her appearance seemed well deserved but what got all the boys at school thought was why that when she had her back toward people, she resembled a beautiful swimsuit model while her front side revealed a nerdy-looking, redheaded braces glittering bookworm of a girl. Her too was aiming to become a psychiatrist but in terms of criminal psychiatry. She was best friends with Karen Hannah and the second rated student in the entire class. And due to no sign of finding where Karen had disappeared to, the principal of the school chosen Carol to do the valedictory speech in her stead.

Carol was already prepared for the ceremony and Jake and the rest had donned their black robe, each of them with a golden collar around their necks. Their mortar board had sat neatly on their heads with their golden tassells hanging on the left side of the board. They would not touch those until they have received their diplomas and their principal gave them the cue. They walked toward the front doors of the gymnasium facing inward while their families and relatives were waiting patiently. And just before the music started, Jason Baker turned his head to his left to where Jake was standing.

"Jake," the big jock whispered. "You're a good guy to push around. So no hard feelings?"

Jake turned toward the giant monster and saw his paw secretly reaching out to him. This was the first time Jason showed some respect to the people below him since it would probably the last time those two will see each other eye to eye. Jake had no excuse to accept this friendly moment, so he shook Jason's hand with grace.

"Let me know when you make it in the football team." Jake whispered back.

"Sure thing. Maybe you could be an excellent mascot." a slight laugh was heard from his foul breath. A mascot to Carlton City's football team, some dream job, Jake thought sarcastically.

The eighth grade musical band started blaring out through their instruments as the song 'Pomp and Circumstance' filled the gymnasium. For the graduates, they would have to walk along with the beat of the music. Right foot forward, left foot joined, left foot forward, right foot joined. They would have to walk like that all the way down the pathway that had split the crowd in two toward a platform of chairs. Most of them tried not to look at their families' proud faces for they may lose the rhythm in the walk. But Jake had glanced at his aunt Laura and his little cousin Becky waving in the middle of the left half of the crowd, but all he had ever thought was seeing his parents standing there waving and smiling at him. Even if they were both gone, he would still see them in the front row facing the stage. He knew that he had made them proud.

Jake glanced at another family he recognized, Karen's parents. Her mother was crying while the father held her in her arms. It was sad that Karen had not been part of the walk, and she would always imagine her precious daughter walking down with her glowing smile. Jake was hoping Karen would be safe and sound since he was just as much of a friend to her as he was with Alice Craig. Jake had silently did a quick prayer in his heart, praying alongside others for Karen to be back home.

As soon as the graduating class arrived at the platform of chairs, each seat had a their names labeled so when they leave, they would go out in the same manner. By the time they sat down and music had finished, the school's principal, Dale Winston walked up to the podium. He was a strict, middle-aged man who also happened to be a bit patriotic. People in town had thought he was using his strict attitude because he wanted to show the school's true nature and purpose, but others believed his strictness was just for show and trying to make an image of himself in front of the public and his superiors. When he spoke into the microphone, the sound of a cross between a leader and a obnoxious foreigner from England boomed through the stage speakers.

"Ladies and gentlemen of Greensburg town." He said valiantly. "I welcome you all to another time of year when our children will be taking an important journey into the world we all know. They will step out of this building with the sense of success in their hearts and filled with opportunities as they venture forth toward their ultimate dream."

Principal Winston liked to hear his own voice as well as having them heard by others. He believed that the entire school acted as the centre of the world, or his world if I one would put it. And that his voice would signify a true sense of academic achievement. In other words, he wanted Greensburg High School to be better than all the others. But basically he just wanted the promotion to superintendent so he can run the schools they way he imagined it. Half of the townspeople admired his dedication, but his intentions were too selfish. He just wanted to be top of the academic world with absolutely no care about the people around him and the students whom they would look up to. And none of them blamed him for it, since his father was like that to him back in England.

"It is with great honour to begin this ceremony with an opening speech from our highest rated student of 2009, Karen Hannah. Unfortunately we all know about her recent disappearance and I pray for her and her family that she would return home safely. So our second-highest rated student and Karen's colleague Carol Graham will be performing the opening speech in which Miss Hannah had prepared for us on this memorable occasion."

Carol Graham stood up from her seat and walked down the metal steps, heading toward the wooden, white painted steps to the stage. Jake took a quick glance at her when she had her back toward her classmates and he was still dumbfounded by her appearance. Smooth looking legs, curvy waist and fine shoulders were key elements of a beauty model. And her small, white shoes with golden butterflies sitting neatly on her ankle strap showed a sign on innocence and pure kindness that completed her personality. It was all heaven for the boys in her class until she reached the podium showing her nerdy-looking visage.

"Families and friends," she spoke lightly in the microphone with slight slurring noise due to her braces. "Since her disappearance, my dear and caring friend, Karen Hannah had written a speech for us all and I will read to you what she had prepared for this important day."

Jake wasn't really paying much attention to the speech that was given out, though he was concentrated on Karen's parents who were sitting, listening to every word that their beloved daughter had written and believed that she would have been proud of Carol to do this job for her. But things started to change when Jake saw a policeman entering the gymnasium. It was the town sheriff's deputy Alan Craig, Alice's brother. He quietly walked up to Karen's parents and whispered something to them. Whatever Alan had said to them, the mother was soaked in more tears then ever and Alan had escorted the Hannah family toward the main doors of the gymnasium.

"What was that about?" Alice whispered to Jake.

"I don't know," he replied. "But I don't think its good news."

"And when the time comes when we are ready for what is ahead of us," Carol continued with the speech as Karen's parents went outside, "we will continue on and strive for a better tomorrow." The crowd applaud with so much grace. Karen's heart and soul was in that speech and Carol had delivered it to the masses. Jake didn't applaud as much since he was still worried about what Alan had told Karen's parents.

"On a final note," Carol continued on, "I would also like to point out..."

Everything had suddenly gone dark. All the lights in the gymnasium were out and the only light source that everyone was able to see was the emergency lights above the main doors and the side doors. One of the teachers had appeared behind the crowd with his hands up in the air.

"It's okay, people!" he yelled out to the crowd. "One of the fuses has blown, we'll have light in no time."

Then the emergency lights had begun slowly to fade out. This school had been known for several power outages and the backup generator for the emergency lights was as old as the Vietnam war. Every time the lights in our classroom would go out, a few of us would cheer and yelled out "Let's get naked!" Most likely Jason Baker would say something like that. Though he did not said anything when the emergency lights had finally gone out a few moments later.

It was completely dark, and no one can see each other, not even the person next to them. A few seconds later a couple of cigarette lighters were lit but it wasn't enough to reveal everyone's faces. There was some mumbling in the crowd and a small sense of panic, but their mumbling had suddenly stopped when a high-pitched scream pierced through their ears. The scream was acute and made everybody's blood turn cold as a block of ice and possibly made certain heart beats skip and almost losing their rhythm. As soon as the lights came back on, everyone was visible. Every person, student and teacher were finally revealed in the light...except for Carol Graham.

Chapter 2

Carol Graham was gone, vanished along with the darkness that had clouded the gymnasium for a short while. The townspeople looked about their surroundings to indicate where she may had disappeared to, but there was no sign of the high school graduate. Even principal Winston, the superintendent and other members of the school's district cannot seem to find Carol anywhere in the gymnasium, not even through the crowd. The townspeople had started to panic a little thinking it may be the same incident that happened with Karen Hannah. Some believed that it was probably just some stunt Carol had pulled or some magic trick. But the only problem was that nobody saw Karen vanished the same way Carol had.

That was what Principal Winston was thinking. Often some students in his school had no respect nor remorse for those who had either loss a loved one nor having no sensitivity to what was happening. Sometimes their imagination had gone way too far then their moral sense. From what he had been taught by his father was that academic studies were more important than one's imagination. He would rather see his son being a businessman and rise along side him than having his head up in the clouds. Sure, it is good to dream of something that you would like to achieve in life, but every time Winston had done that, his father would smack him on the head with a Accounting text book. After he died, he felt somewhat relieved but all of his aggressive ways of getting him to be like his father only made him half of what his father was, a sneering, strict, but a mellow dreamer. He had a dream of becoming a teacher one time. And all of the abusive, hard-as-nails, strictness that had been passed on to him from his father made him achieve that dream and even more. He became a principal in a short time and he was so close of getting a promotion to superintendent. While the previous superintendent was about to retire in the fall, after the graduation of Greensburg High School.

Winston kept looking around and about for any sign of where Carol Graham might be. He wasn't able to spot her, not even from the balcony above the mumbling audience. But something had caught his eye, on the floor from where she was standing. Her mortar board hat was found laying upside down but had really struck his eye was what was underneath it.

Jake was still looking around also thinking Carol may have pulled a stunt or a magic trick. Then he thought that if it would be a magic trick, there would have been a trap door on the stage floor behind the podium somewhere. It sort of made sense to when Carol would have vanished that quickly under the darkness the gymnasium had briefly fallen under, so he turned his scanning eyes toward the stage and where Carol was standing. There was definitely something there, but from the assigned seat to where Jake had sat and the viewing angel that would hid a person's legs behind the podium made it difficult for him to see if there was any clue. All he was able to see was Carol's mortar board hat laying upside down. He even stood up and just by standing on his toes, there was something underneath the hat. He still could not see much but he barely saw a something black underneath. It was definitely not the same light-brownish colour the rest of the stage floor had.

Winston stood up from his chair from the back of the stage and slowly walked up to where the mortar board had laid. As he gotten closer, the black stain, that looked like it had burned right through the varnished floor, became more clear. And the complete view of the stain had almost shook Winston in his leather shoes. The stain had formed a shape, a silhouette of a person burned right into the stage floor. After lifting the mortar board hat from the floor, there was even a black line sitting on top of the silhouette that may have been the hat itself. After better view of the picture, it became frightening clear that the silhouette was indeed belonged to Carol Graham. It was neatly placed and formed perfectly as if Carol would still be standing behind the podium, still giving the valedictory speech.

Deputy Alan Craig rushed back into the gymnasium assuming he heard Carol's blood-curdling scream. He quickly looked around crowd for any sign of her but there was none. As we quickly ran up toward the stage, he too saw the black silhouette on the stage floor, neatly shaped and positioned directly where Carol had stood. Seeing that sparked the time where he and a few other officers were searching Karen's bedroom the night she vanished. She had also left a black silhouette on the bedroom floor behind her desk, perfectly shaped as if she would still be sitting there. Only thing that went through his mind after was hoping he would not find what he had recently found back Karen's house.

So, without any further hesitation, Alan went up to the podium and spoke to the civilians of Greensburg.

"Ladies and gentlemen." he spoke. "Please remain calm. The Greensburg police will handle this situation and notify you if there is any news. I would strongly advise to return to your homes and lock your doors for the time being."

The crowd slowly turned toward the main doors of the gymnasium and walked out of the school building.

"As for the graduates of 2009," he continued, "your diplomas will be delivered to your doors personally after a short talk with your principal. Thank you for your cooperation and congratulations to you all." he finished by giving a smiling wink to her sister Alice who was sitting next to Jake. He was really proud of her sister and promised to give her some support when she goes to University in Carlton City to become a fashion designer.

Alice was already proud of her older brother for handling the crowd that easily, but can never be more proud than the day the town made him into an officer of the law, a deputy at the most. He was also a good friend to Jake. The two young men got along so well that they were almost like brothers, but back in junior high, Alan was always there to help him out. That was all because of the bully and Alice's boyfriend, Jason Baker.

Jason was always pushing Jake around, not just because of Alice but because he could. The hulking fan of many sports had dreams of becoming an athlete went way over his head that most of the time he pretend himself to be a sports star and anybody who was weaker than him were all nothing but a bunch of sacs of dough. And whenever Jake got in contact with him, whether it was smack talk or fists Alan somehow stepped in and prevent Jason from doing any damage. Though he cannot figure out the reason why Alice was dating him, but anyone who was friend of Alice was also a friend of him. As soon as he made it into the police force, he kept his eye on Jason to make sure he didn't harassed his best friend or he would have to place him handcuffs. According to Alice, Jason may be a hot headed, overly protective sports jockey, but he did have a soft spot because of her kindness and loving spirit that she had shown to him. He actually imagined Alice as his cheerleader but her mind was already set on being a fashion designer. But hey, even fashion designers can make awesome clothing for cheerleaders. She even promised him that if she made one cheerleader outfit, she would probably wear it sometime in their honeymoon. If there would be a honeymoon, of course.

Jake and the others followed the townspeople out of the main doors of the gymnasium and outside the building into the morning sun. It was hard to believe that the whole thing that happened in there occurred in a short time span and to think that the graduation ceremony would end with Carol's disappearance right in front of the public. Jake's aunt and cousin were waiting at the car near the parking lot just outside school.

"Wow." she said to her nephew. "First Karen, now Carol?" She shook her head in disbelief.

"Well, I think we may know something about Karen soon." Jake said. "Just before the black out, I saw Alan talked to her parents and her mother looked upset than ever."

"Yeah, I saw that too. Doesn't look like good news at all. Well, I hope they have better luck with Carol and find out whats actually happening."

"Me too. We should head back home."

Aunt Laura Miller smiled at Jake.

"I got cake waiting for you and Becky's anxious to eat a piece right now."

Becky was sitting in the backseat of the car poking her cheeks through the window.

"Yeah, I can't stay cute forever, you know."

Jake laughed at her smart comment and peered through the opening of the half-way downed window.

"I'll see if I can persuade your mom to give you a big piece."

Jake and his aunt both got into their car and drove home. As soon as they arrived, Jake took off his robe and his mortar board hat and threw it on living room sofa. He then noticed a cake that was sitting in the middle of the dining room table. The cake was made of two golden layers with peanut butter in between, while the whole caked was soaked with chocolate frosting. Around the edge of the top layer was green swirls with white lettering in the middle to which it read "Congrats, Jake! GH Graduate of 2009."

Jake smiled as if the cake had just spoke those words to him but it was his Aunt Laura and his cousin Becky who put their heart and soul into baking it and he couldn't be any happier. The last time he felt this happy was when his father came to visit him and his mother on his sixth birthday. Every time Detective Jeremy Miller would appear at the front door of the old house Jake and his mother moved into, little Jake would run into his father arms. As for his mother Olivia, the sight of seeing those two together almost brought a tear in one of her eyes but she kept on wishing it would stay like that forever. If only Jeremy would have moved with them, or at least transfer his job to the Greensburg Police Department, they would live together as a family again peacefully and protect his family at the same time. But unfortunately, her efforts of persuading her husband were in vain.

Jeremy had brought something from the city, a birthday present for Jake. The size of the package was taller than the three-foot-six birthday boy. When he tore the red gift wrapping like a starving, ravaging hyena with his mutilated meal, his eyes suddenly widened with surprise and excitement. It was a red coloured fishing rod which included a bobbing ball with a cartoon scuba-diver designed on it. Jake gave his father another big hug and he promised to his son that by the time he goes on vacation, he would take him and his wife camping at the Greensburg Nature Campground located in the far East of the town and be able to go fishing at the nearby river. The first day of his vacation was also his and Olivia's eighth wedding anniversary, but it was also the day of when Olivia received the phone call from the station in Carlton City that her husband was shot and killed on the freeway, on his way to see his family.

"Go ahead, Jake." his aunt Laura said, disrupting his moment in memory lane. "You get to eat the first piece. I gotta make a few phone calls."

"Okay," Jake said. "Thanks a lot, Aunt Laura."

Little Becky poked Jake's side with a proud smile.

"I did the writing."

He padded his little cousin on the head.

"Well I have to thank you for that, Becky."

Much later after, Jake was in his room after having dinner with his relatives. He laid on his bed looking into mind and tried to make sense of all that was happening. Karen's disappearance, then Carol's. That was strangest thing that ever occurred since the last time Greensburg had reported some missing children which happened about two months earlier, almost after the wife of the Chemistry teacher was killed in the freeway accident. Ten children, all girls between age of eight and twelve had gone missing and there had been no progress in finding their whereabouts or any clue to where they had gone. It started with just one girl, then two twin sisters, and other followed after almost one or two of them each week. The numbers stopped growing sometime during the spring and the police even had help from other departments outside including Carlton City. The police had almost lost hope townspeople had never gave up on the missing children so they had to do what they can in their power to find them all while trying to enjoy their lives as each passing day moved on.

Jake looked on his night table next to his bed and noticed a small picture frame of him and his parents. That was the day when his mother Olivia and he moved into their new home and it was the first time his father came from the city for a weekend visit. He was sitting on his mother's lap and his father behind the chair with his hands on her shoulders. They all looked happy together, despite the fact that Jeremy had to stay in the city because of his job as a police detective. His aunt Laura had been the one taking the photograph and the flower-designed wooden frame was made by little Becky on his fifteenth birthday.

"You miss them a lot, don't you?" she said standing at the foot of his bed.

"Yeah, I really do. I miss them a lot."

"I don't know much about your mommy, but my mommy told me she was a good person."

Jake lightly smiled while his eyes were still fixated on the photo. The memorable moment was interrupted by his aunt calling him from underneath.

"Jake," she called out. "Alan's here to see you."

Jake placed the frame back on his night table and quickly got off the bed.

"At least you still have us." Becky said smiling.

"Right you are, squirt." Jake said petting Becky's little head.

Becky didn't like to be called a squirt because of the fact that she was small, so her smile turned into a cute little frown.

"I'm not a squirt." she said sharply, almost raising her voice.

Jake stopped mid track and looked back at his cousin with a smirk on his face.

"Okay, okay. You're a little squirt."

"I'm not little." Becky's voice raised a bit more in anger, but Jake had already disappeared through the stairway from his bedroom.

When he reached the bottom, Jake noticed deputy Alan Craig was standing near the doorway talking to his aunt.

"Hey, Alan." he said feeling glad to see his old friend.

"Hey there, buddy." Alan spoke back with a proud smile. "Just came to deliver you your diploma. Sorry about the whole ceremony being cut short but congratulations anyways."

"Thanks. So any news about what happened?"

"Not much, I'm afraid. We've asked the people around town if they had seen Carol outside the school since the power outage and still no clue. But what we are hoping for is to not have her ended up like Karen."

What Alan said sparked something in Jake's mind. He remembered seeing Alan walking in during the speech and told Karen's parents something and made Mrs. Hannah more upset than ever.

"Yeah," Jake said. "You just happened to talked with her parents before the lights went out and you were escorting them out."

"We had to have them identify the body we found. It was mostly a skeleton covered in some form of black goop. Possibly some oil-based compound. They've already confirmed that it was their daughter due to the fact that her body was wearing a golden crucifix her mother have given her during the Grad Mass."

The mass for graduates occurred five days before Karen's reported disappearance. Jake was at the mass as well since his aunt Laura had kept bugging him about it. And he did remember Alice Craig saying about going to see Pastor Brian Mayne for something.

"That's terrible." Laura said somewhat shocked by the entire thing. "Who would do such a thing to girl like Karen?"

"Well, like I said." Alan continued. "We're doing our job as best as we can to make sure Carol doesn't end up like that."

Jake then thought of something that he also had seen at the gymnasium.

"Wait," he said. "Wasn't there some sort of black stain on the stage floor, from where Carol was standing?"

Alan had wished Jake didn't asked that question since the incident was similar to Karen's case, but he clearly remembered seeing it after running back into the gymnasium upon hearing the graduate student scream.

"Yeah, there was." Alan said softly. "The life-sized black stain was found there. And luckily the stage also has a couple of storage compartments in the front for maintenance and we didn't have to break the floorboards. Carol wasn't even under there. You can say she completely vanished."

Alan slowly turned toward the door away from the confused faces Jake and Laura had on. He then sparked an idea and looked back quickly with a slight smile.

"Since Karen's funeral is tomorrow in the evening, how about if I treat you something for lunch at the diner?"

Jake's confused expression had disappeared.

"Sure, that would be great."

"Alice wanted to meet us there too. She's got some more fashion sketches she wanted to show us and to bring to the University this fall."

"Sure, I'll be there."

Alan was almost half-way out through the door when Jake suddenly stopped him for one last question in which the answer had sent chills up his spine.

"Alan," he stopped the young deputy . "Where did you find Karen's body?"

There was a slight silence and Alan gave out the details of how one of the deputies was doing a routine check around Karen's house the same morning in case they may have overlooked something. He was walking around with a cup of coffee in his hand surveying the place and end up thinking that he should be home watching the game on television. The deputy stopped in the living room for another look when he did not noticed that something had fallen in his coffee cup. He turned back and was about to take another sip when he tasted something that made the muscles in his face tightened, his eyes squinting, his throat squeaking and felt like he was gonna throw up. It tasted foul, and he even received a smell that stank like something had puked into his coffee, mixed it with crude oil and sweetened with something that was ice-cold and spoiled rotten.

When he spat out whatever he had in his mouth, the instant reaction of his head bending forward had delivered his eyes to something that was on the living room carpet between his feet. There was a small, black stain on the carpet. And when the deputy bent down for a closer look and touched the stain, it was wet and it looked like a small pool. Suddenly, a black drop had passed by his eyes from above. Looking up to where the drop had came from, there was a bit more of the black liquid on the ceiling and one floor above the living room was Karen's bedroom.

"The deputy called me and Sheriff Barkley to check it out." Alan continued his story. "When we arrived, we noticed that the source of the black substance was right where that life-sized stain was found on bedroom floor. So, we took an axe from out patrol vehicle and broke through it."

Jake just stood there nearly frozen. "You mean..."

"Yes," Alan said quietly. "With no point of entry or any sign of physical force whatsoever, covered in that same substance..." There was another pause. "Karen was found between her bedroom floor and the living room ceiling."

Chapter 3

The morning, summer sun enlightened Greensburg with its bright and warm rays. The light had filled the roads with life and energy, like as if the entire world had just been reborn. Cars driving up and down the streets, people walking by in their summer hats, children playing and laughing as drops of water soaked their skin from a waving sprinkler nestled on their front lawns. The campgrounds outside the town were filled and tourists walked along several nature trails and pathways. It was a beautiful summer day filled with warmth from the sun and a cool breeze to keep the people from overheating. Some say it was because the heavens were smiling and this was their reward for constant hard work and strain that the people below had to endure to keep everything in order. But some say the heavens were smiling over one particular person pushing a grocery kart in the Greensburg Food Market.

Olivia Chambers Miller had a slight smile on her face. A hint of joy and excitement had filled her heart and her soul for when she heard the news about her husband Jeremy. It was their eighth wedding anniversary, and Jeremy had planned to visit his family for the weekend and take them on a camping trip. It was also the prefect time for their son Jake to try out the new fishing pole his father had got him on his sixth birthday.

"Hey, Olivia!" a woman called out from behind the vegetable isle.

"Hey, Laura." Olivia Miller waved back from the dairy department as she watched Laura pushed her grocery kart toward her sister's.

"How have you been?"

"I'm doing good. Just excited about tonight."

"Really?"

"Yeah, but I think Jake is more excited than I am."

"Let me guess, Jeremy is coming down on your anniversary."

"That's right. He's taking a few days of vacation so we can have one night together. Then tomorrow he's gonna take all of us camping for the weekend."

"Oh, that's just great." Laura said happily. "I'm sure like to take another picture of all of you on your camping trip."

"You should come with us, Laura. It'll be fun."

Laura gave a somewhat disappointed look. "I wish I could but I have to fill in for someone over the weekend. But I will take that picture for sure. Seeing you all together always seemed to brighten my day."

Laura had a wonderful job at the Greensburg Civic Centre. She basically was in charge of certain arrangements which involved sport events, swimming classes, even certain therapeutic sessions for the elderly. But over the weekend, she would have to help with some maintenance around the area along with her boyfriend, who's partner that was suppose to help him had recently been struck by the flu.

"Just seeing Jeremy and our son together always brighten mine. You know how Jeremy likes to talk detective stories to him like he'd be today's Sherlock Holmes."

"Have you ever imagine Jake as a detective?" Laura asked.

"Sometimes, but not in a city like where Jeremy is." Olivia's smile dissolved into slight sadness.

Laura thought of something that she wanted to tell Olivia but she didn't want to scare her. She recently heard something in the radio about some gang riot that was happening in the city and almost every police precinct in Carlton City as well as Jeremy's precinct were involved in stopping them. They even got some help from the Greensburg's police and even some from the United States since there was talk that some gang members, whom were Americans, had used fake passports to cross the border. She didn't want to alarm her but Laura had prayed for Olivia's husband to arrive safely.

"Well," Laura said gathering her items in her grocery kart. "I might as well take off. You have fun this weekend. And let me know when your leaving for your camping trip so I can take the photo."

"Sure thing. Bye, Laura." Olivia said as her sister pushed her kart toward the cashier.

Having Jeremy visiting for the weekend felt like her knight in shining armour was on a quest to take the princess to an enchanted forest. It has been a long time since her family had spend quality time together, especially on occasions like a camping trip. The last time they went somewhere was at a baseball game across the US border, south of Carlton City. It wasn't a long trip from Canada to the US since it was only a three-hour drive to the game. But the whole family enjoyed the tensity of the baseball game, whether it was from waiting for the pitch, cracking sound of the bat that made the ball flew just like a bird that had eaten some worms that may have been filled with rocket fuel, and finally seeing the batter jumping for joy, throwing his hat in the air all the way to the home base after the ball went over the fence for the home run. The crowd cheered so gratefully to the winning home team and so did Jake and his parents. They had so much fun together, and it was memory that they would never forget. But that was before Olivia decided to take Jake and move out of that violent and corrupted city into a peaceful, quiet town.

Later, after Olivia paid her groceries and was storing them in her car, a police patrol car drove into the parking space next to her. The driver door swung open and a brown cowboy hat emerged from the car, following by small brown eyes, pointed nose, a curly Hungarian-style moustache with a fuzzy grin. It was Greensburg's own town sheriff Clarence Barkley, in his mid-thirties and a long time friend and former partner to Carlton City's detective, Jeremy Miller. He had been in the police force for ten years, most of the time as Jeremy's partner. During that time he was getting weary with the amount of crime the city had been infested with, and decided to transfer to Greensburg which from his opinion, the best choice he had done. He enjoyed the quiet, country life as much as Olivia did, but it would have been a lot better if Jeremy would have done the same thing as Clarence had done.

"Morning, Olivia." the sheriff said, nearly showing pearly whites through his thin smile.

"Hi, Sheriff Barkley." Olivia greeted him back with the same smile.

"How you and your son making out?"

"Oh, we're holding out just fine, thanks. Just excited about tonight."

Barkley remembered it all too well. "Oh, that's right. You and Jeremy's wedding anniversary."

"Not only that, he's gonna take us and Jake on a camping trip for the weekend."

"Now that sound like fun. I used go camping at those campgrounds with my daughter when I was living in Carlton City. Best time we've had, I assure you."

"How is your daughter?"

"Oh, she's doing fine at the University. One more year and she can open up her own hair saloon right here."

Olivia's smile slowly faded away, thinking of how her husband would do well living in Greensburg, just like Sheriff Barkley was. Barkley noticed that semi-sad expression on her and understand why Jeremy didn't move with his family.

"Listen, Olivia." Clarence said softly as he looked into the young woman's sad eyes. "Jeremy's a fine cop and a good friend and all. I'm pretty sure he has good reason to stay in Carlton City. Just sometimes I wonder where his priorities are. I even told him myself about you folks moving in, but he seems to proud of his job. He really thinks by staying at a city like that could make a difference. Well, sure, *some* difference. But it doesn't erase the fact he has a family on his side that needs him."

Olivia stored the last of her groceries and closed the trunk, showing a small sign of anger. "If he really wants to make a difference, he should start with his family, first."

"I know what you mean." Clarence started to walk, heading toward the front doors of the market. "Well, I hope you have fun this weekend. I'll see ya later."

Both Olivia and the sheriff shared a nod as Clarence walked away. But his heart nearly skipped a beat when the radio attached to his right side screeched following by a female voice.

"Sheriff Barkley, this is dispatch. Come in, over?" the radio barked.

Barkley grabbed the microphone that was strapped onto his left shoulder.

"This is Sheriff Barkley, over?"

"The department in Carlton City is requesting immediate assistance involving a gang riot. They even called in other departments around the area including one from across the US border."

Barkley made a face, signified that he won't be getting his spare ribs and chicken for dinner.

"Copy that, dispatch. I'm on my way."

Olivia only caught pieces of the conversation from within her car, something about Carlton City and a gang riot. But then she shook her head and ignored the whole thing thinking it was just a normal police matter. If there was something going on in Carlton City then her husband would be at the spot but she was hoping he would arrive in Greensburg soon. She had no time to think about it all, so she started her car and drove home.

The house was small and livable but warm and cozy enough to keep anybody safe from the harsh weather. The interior walls were a reddish colour, vibrant and relaxing as the floors were grayish white with a tint of yellow showing in between the zigzag pattern. The living room had a couch big enough for Olivia's family to sit together in front of the television and watching animated films with a recliner for when Jeremy decided to relax and read a book, or just taking a short nap.

Olivia walked in through the front door with her grocery bags and placed them on the island counter in the kitchen. By the time she started unpacking them she heard little footsteps coming down the stairs from between the kitchen and living room.

"Morning, Jake." she said to the owner of those little footsteps.

"Hi, mommy." the six-year-old Jake Miller said cheerfully. "What did you get me?"

His mother laughed.

"Well, I got you your chocolate cereal. You might as well eat some since you looked like you got out of bed."

Jake got out of bed with bed-hair. The hair behind his head was pressed upward as well as some on the left side. It must be some kind of crazy dream, she thought. He had always told his mother how he dreams about becoming a famous detective like his father, or at least like the ones in his books. Solving crimes, putting pieces of a puzzle together using logic. And he and his father would watch detective films and TV shows together on weekends.

Olivia could easily tell that her son was proud of his father being a detective, but being a detective is not the same as what you would see on TV or read in fictional books. It could affect your personal life, sometimes it could be dangerous, scary and horrible. Especially when you're talking about a homicide detective, in which Jake's father's job was.

"You excited about tomorrow?" Olivia asked her son with warm grin.

"Yeah," little Jake said with enthusiasm. "I wanna try out the fishing pole so bad that I was gonna go fishing in the bathtub.

Olivia laughed again.

"Well a bathtub is a good idea to show how it works, but it's a lot better when your at the river. Your dad will teach you how to but bait on the hook, cast the line and reel it in as soon as you feel a nibble."

Jake took a quick glance at his new fishing pole, still in its package on the floor leaning against the side of the stairs, waiting for its owner to open it up and claim it.

"This is gonna be the best weekend ever," he said with more enthusiasm.

Olivia took a quick glance at his son, seeing the excitement in his face. Just for the fact they both missed Jeremy since they moved to Greensburg, it would be a memory to cherish for all of their lives for eternity. She smiled a bit seeing how her family would be together again for on weekend but she only wished they would be together forever.

Later in the afternoon, Olivia was fixing her hair and applied some perfume for the special night she was gonna have with her husband, on their wedding anniversary. She was also wearing a blue dress in which she wore it on their first anniversary and a golden necklace that she got as a gift when she graduated from high school. She applied make-up, lip gloss and then she was finally looking glamorous and ready to have a fun night.

The telephone attached to the wall between the kitchen and the front door had rung. It was Laura that called, saying she would watch over Jake while both her sister and Jeremy spend their night out and was about to rent some movies. Jake had thought it was his father so he nearly ran down the stairs and stopped about near the bottom when his mother said it was his aunt. But instead of walking back upstairs he sat on one of the steps and decided to wait for either his aunt or his father to walk in through the door. Few hours later, nearly around 4:30pm, a car drove into the drive way and Laura had emerged from the vehicle. Jake nearly thought it was his father but the white car wasn't his. Jeremy's car was a black sports car that came with a sunroof and square headlights hidden in the hood that would flip upright with a push of a button.

Laura walked in through the door looking around for any sign of her brother-in-law.

"He's not here yet?" Laura asked her sister.

"He'll show up soon," Olivia replied. "Knowing Jeremy, he never missed an anniversary."

"Hey, Aunt Laura." Jake waved from the stairs with a innocent smile.

"Hey there, big guy. Just rented some movies and got some popcorn for both of us."

Laura was carrying a small sack loaded with a box of popcorn and a DVD rental entitled 'Billy the Blind Bat Mysteries: The Upside-downed Earth.' It was from a popular cartoon that Jake watched on television every Saturday morning and he won't watch a single episode without his 'Billy the Blind Bat' hat and mask. Jake would laugh every time the animated bat would fly into walls, transparent windows and gets into crazy situations while solving a mystery, all because the bat was blind.

An hour went by and Jeremy had not arrived. Things were slowly going through Olivia's head such as what may have delayed his arrival, but she tried to ignore those thoughts and forcing herself to be a bit more positive. She sat at the dining table waiting and took several glances at the clock on the microwave. It read 5.37pm and there was still no sign of Jeremy's black sports car. He had never missed a single wedding anniversary and he would never give up the chance to see his wife and son at all. But sometimes, when your a member of the police force, your own job could steal that chance away just a sound of phone call or the screeching of their radios that tells you that you have a job to do. Your job is to serve and protect Carlton City, maintaining peace among its walls and provide help and support for the people within those walls. Those were running through her thoughts when the sun had set and the fact that Jeremy would not move in with his family because he was too proud of his job had angered her, she felt some disappointment and received the feeling of being stood up by her own beloved husband.

"I'm gonna go upstairs and lay down for a while." Olivia bluntly said as she got up from her dining room chair and began to walk upstairs. Laura watched her sister's sad face from the couch, sitting next to Jake as she disappeared into the dim-lit hallway at the top of the stairs. She felt sorry and hoped that she can do anything, but she couldn't think of anything at all.

The telephone rang shortly after. Olivia heard the phone from her bedroom as she was lying down on her bed looking up in the ceiling where the old ceiling lamp was hanging crookedly. She was trying to think things over and she even had thought of getting a divorce, but her train of thought was interrupted when Laura called her from downstairs saying the phone call was hers. She got downstairs and grabbed the receiver from Laura's hands.

"Hello?" she spoke in the microphone.

Laura can barely hear the mumbled voice from the ear piece but she knew the voice was not Jeremy's but the captain of the Carlton City Police Department.

"What?" she said, as she tried to made clear onto what the captain on the other line had told her. To her, it sounded absurd and almost impossible.

A few seconds later, her breathing had slowly began to get heavy and a slight tremble in her arms was barely noticeable. After hearing more of what the captain had said over the phone, her breathing became even more heavier and her eyes slowly began to water. She tried to speak, but the sudden pain in her heart was stopping her and she was unable to let out a single word. Even when she attempted to mouth it out, there wasn't a single voice that had escaped from her soul. She was barely choking and her right hand had went up to her gaping mouth, trying cover what may be a faint cry. The more she heard, the more worse she had got and her warm tears had finally begun to run down her rouged cheekbones.

She heard a click in the ear piece. The conversation was over, and Olivia had slowly hung up the phone as Laura watched her sister's heart, through her facial expression, torn apart by the news she had received. Olivia fell into Laura's arms and began bawling. In between her cries she was able to say the name of her husband once. As for Jake who sat quietly on the couch, he watched the whole thing happened right before his eyes. He watched her mother's heart breaking into pieces and her beautiful smile that she always wore had been melted away by running tears. Her calm, comforting voice had been distorted, and disrupted by the cries she had made but muffled into his aunt's arms. He just sat there watching his mother crying loudly and when he heard her saying his father's name, he knew something bad had happened to him. He too began to breathe heavily and almost had a tear running down his cheek. But before he actually cried, he called out to his father in plain emptiness, as if he had faded away right before his teary, hazel eyes.

"Daddy?"

Chapter 4

Jake opened his eyes. His first thoughts that ran through his head was that he wished he had not dreamed about that night, when his mother received the phone call saying his father was killed in a convenient store by a drive-by gang, heading toward town to see his wife and son, on his wedding anniversary. He stood there underneath the bed sheets for a few minutes, regaining the rest of his thoughts and consciousness until he remembered something. He was going to meet Alice and Alan at the diner for lunch, that day. But still, even though he could remember the phone call, he still could not remember anything that happened before the night his mother hung herself. Even if that was just a small memory, even if lasted an hour or so, he still felt there was something missing in his mind. Like someone had taken a book and just removed a single page or maybe a whole chapter and casted it into the dark depths of his mind.

Jake finally got out of bed and walked downstairs. He saw his aunt Laura making breakfast and little Becky, eating her cereal and reading her comics, just like that morning on his graduation day. Only one thing different was the enthusiasm wasn't there, just a small sign of mourning and sympathy.

Of course, he thought. Not only he had to meet Alice and Alan at the diner, but Karen Hannah's funeral was going to be held later in that evening.

"Morning, Jake." his aunt said to her descending nephew, noticing a plain expression on his face, like as if he hadn't woke up right. "You okay?"

Jake nodded.

"Just had one of those dreams, about the phone call." Then he slightly shook his head. "It's funny. I can remember Mom receiving the phone call about Dad, but I cannot seem to remember much of anything before she hung herself."

"Well, whatever it was," his aunt said trying to cover some sadness from the loss of her sister. "I'm pretty sure it's nothing important. Your mom did went under some heavy depression, heavy enough she didn't even left a note."

Laura placed some pancakes on the table, dripping with sweet maple syrup and melted butter.

"Well, might as well eat your pancakes before Becky starts chomping them down herself."

Jake slightly laughed and glanced at his little cousin, still glued to her comic book assuming she wasn't paying attention.

"Oh, and after your done having lunch with your friends, there's some things I want you to pick up at the market for me. We may have a few visitors after Karen's funeral."

Jake made quirky smirk thinking why did get stuck with doing errands. But when his aunt gave him a small piece of paper with only three items on it, he felt some relief. He folded the list, stuffed it in his right pocket of his jeans and went straight in to the pancakes.

They were homemade pancakes made with buckwheat flower, and the syrup that glazed all over was made at the Greensburg Sugar Camp, which was nestled in the middle of the camp grounds, and an hour walk away from the camp's tourist attraction, The Black Cave. He remembered going there with his parents one time during the winter. The sweet, sugary smell from the evaporator inside a giant shed had flooded the camp grounds as the steam from the machine poured out of the chimney, warming up the cold bodies of anyone who walked by it. And when the syrup was made, the workers placed wooden sticks on the snow and poured the syrup on them so that the snow would stick to the syrup and cool off. When it was ready, snow-covered maple syrup on a stick. It was a perfect way to taste test it and Jake and his parents enjoyed it to the very last.

In between summer and fall, Jake's father would take him to The Black Cave, which happened to be part of Greensburg's heritage. The forest ranger that gave them the tour said that the reason it was called 'the Black Cave' was because the interior of the cave was so dark that no source of light could illuminate the walls. No flashlight, no flare, not even a bonfire. That discovery was founded by the father of Greensburg's pastor, Timothy Mayne. And all of his discoveries and history behind it was recorded and could be found in the town's library. They were the only times Jake had spent with his family before he and his mother moved out.

Later, near noon, Jake walked out of the house and gotten a hint of bright sunshine on his face. Cars drove up and down the streets, the town's citizens walking by, some of them were waving at Jake. It was like another fine day for everyone but there was something in the air. There was a hint of sadness, sympathy and mourning on their faces, all because of Karen's funeral was to be held later in the evening and the townspeople were already preparing themselves for it. Among the walking pedestrians were Karen's parents and the mother and father of Carol Graham. They were seen near the Greensburg Food Market conversing sympathies and hopes to each other in a quiet manner. They had both lost their daughters but only one of them had her kind, bright and innocent soul taken away from them. Snatched away in a blink of an eye, just to leave nothing but her fleshless remains, hidden neatly underneath her bedroom floor, covered in black slime with no force, nor any sign of disturbance.

It was terrible for her parents to find their baby girl in that state and they had wished that the Greensburg Police Department would find the culprit who did this to her and bring Carol back. There was nothing both families of the two Greensburg High School graduates could do, except sit, wait, pray and hope. Even Jake himself had wished, prayed and hoped for Carol to come back home safely and to not to end up like Karen.

Jake began to walk toward the diner. As he walked past a few telephone poles and stores, he noticed a few 'Missing Person' fliers posted on them with the graduation picture of Carol Graham. Though it was just like any other flier since the ones he saw involved missing children, ten of them, girls of between ages eight and twelve. Missing for several months and Carol became next.

Jake didn't stop to look at the fliers, since he thought if he looked at them long enough, his negative thoughts of Carol being in a coffin next to Karen's would take over his mind. So he kept a positive mind and kept telling himself that Carol would show up sooner or later, alive and well and kept that nerdy face and sexy body. Jake slightly shook his head, letting out a small gust of laughter while still trying figure out the combination of Carol's looks.

The Greensburg Diner had welcomed Jake with jingle sound of the bell above the doorway. The interior had a mixture of 80s retro and modern decor, and to kept the 80s style, the diner had an old jukebox which was modified to play compact discs and MP3 files through a laptop computer wired behind the box and through the wooden wall. The bar counter itself had a line of neon lights attached on the white front. The stools were stainless steel with the cushions coloured bright red. The counter had a dark finish with small coloured triangles and small white dots, but the surface was sleek and smooth, good enough to slide glasses and dishes toward a waiting customer. The waitress behind the counter, Betty Schultz had been working at the diner for a long time and knew Jake's mother well. She used to work with Betty as a dishwasher since her husband died but the manager had to fire her because her depression was taking over her job performance.

"Hi, Jake!" Betty said happily, after she heard Jake walked in. "Congrats on your graduation."

"Thanks." Jake said as he looked around the diner for any sign of Alice or Alan.

Alice was sitting in a corner of the diner looking at something that was in a red portfolio. She had a small, brown, bag which was used as a reusable shopping bag, filled with folders and books. Alice looked up from the portfolio and saw Jake standing near the front door and waved at him.

"Over here, Jake." she said, still wearing the same, beautiful smile that Jake had always admired.

Jake went closer to Alice and looked around her. He would assumed that her boyfriend, Jason Baker would be with her since he was still overprotective of his girl.

"Big Jason not with you?" he asked.

"Nah, don't worry." she replied, nearly laughed. "He had to go meet the football coach up in Carlton City, to see if he can tryout for the team. He'll be back in time for the funeral."

Jake sat in front of Alice with his arms on the table.

"What you got there?" he asked.

"This is what I've been working on before graduation, and something to show to the big heads at the Carlton City University."

Alice handed over the red portfolio to Jake. It was filled with pages of sketches, detailing faceless mannequins wearing colourful clothing in a certain pattern that may not be found in any fashion magazine. Jake was surprised by Alice's ideas of different patterns, shapes and fabrics that would make a good outfit for classy parties, banquets, costumes for stage plays and business clothing.

"Wow," Jake said with wide eyes. "This is really something. I mean since I have known you, I've already knew you have such talent but this..."

"You think it's too much?" she asked with a certain look, hoping to get some kind of negative feedback.

"Are you kidding? I mean I may not be a woman nor having interest in women's clothing, but this is truly remarkable. You've really outdone yourself this time"

"Aw, thanks." Alice nearly blushed when she heard the compliments.

There was a knock on the nearby window. Jake and Alice turned toward the sound and noticed it was her brother, deputy Alan, making a funny face with his tongue sticking out. Alice nearly had the urge of taking the pamphlet attached to the tray of salt and pepper shakers and slapped the window, trying to knock that silly face out like a fly. But Alan had already removed his face from the window and made the little bell in the doorway ring.

"Hey, guys." Alan said with a smirk. Then he looked at Jake. "Hey, buddy. Didn't anybody taught you not to look through women's things?"

"Yeah," Jake replied with his own returning smirk while flashing Alice's red portfolio. "But I'm making this as an exception."

They both laughed as Alan sat next to her sister and took a g at the sketches that she had done on those white sheets, neatly organized in her red portfolio.

"She really does have talent, doesn't she?" he said, feeling proud of her little sister and what she might accomplish in the near future.

"She sure does." Jake said, also showing the same expression as Alice blushed even more by their compliments.

"And when are you gonna design some new uniforms for us police?" he asked as he turned his head toward the future fashion designer. "Cause these ones are just boring, and sometimes a bit itchy."

Alice laughed.

"That's for the government to decide. Though I could design a good dress for you."

Alan put his hand up to halt the idea.

"I think I'll stick with the uniform."

The plump and kind waitress arrived at their table with a giant notepad in her left hand and a small pencil in her left.

"What will it be, kids?" Betty asked.

"Burgers and fries for me and Alan with large sodas." Alice ordered.

"And you Jake? What will you be having? The usual?"

"Oh yes, please." Jake replied with his favourite meal in mind. "A nice big plate of poutine and a large soda as well."

"Coming right up"

Whenever Jake visited the diner, he had always ordered some Canadian poutine for lunch. French fries sprinkled heavily with shredded mozzarella cheese and soaked in Betty's homemade gravy. His mother had asked if will he ever get tired of eating poutine. He said no, because it was Betty's homemade gravy that made him coming back for more.

"Anyways," Alan said, "I ran into a little trouble a few hours ago."

"Oh?" Alice said.

"You remember Old Man Peterson? We arrested him for disturbing the peace."

"What did he do this time?" Jake asked.

"He was standing in the middle of the street shouting and screaming that the world is going to end. You could tell he was drunk cause he was holding a bottle of whiskey."

"A crazy old fart drunk out of his mind, eh?" Jake briefly joked.

"Well, it's not like he will do any harm to anyone. Around the same week when Karen was reported missing, someone walked by and saw Peterson fell off a tree an landed on his bicycle with minor fracture oh his back."

"Oh, don't you mention that old pervert!" Betty yelled from the kitchen overhearing the conversation. Betty reappeared with plates of fries and burgers and one plate of poutine for her customers. "That Peterson deserved to be locked up in jail, or maybe at a nut house!"

"Why is that?" Alice asked.

"Well, on that same week, I was getting ready to go to the movies with my husband until I head a crashing noise. When I looked out of my window, there was old Peterson on the ground at the base of the tree, on top of his bicycle. I noticed he had a pair of binoculars in his hand so I assumed he was peeping in my bedroom. That man has no respect for a woman's privacy. Not even a slight of dignity!"

"Calm down, Mrs. Schultz," the young deputy said. "He's in one of our cells, and with that back of his, I don't think he will be climbing any more trees."

"I hope you are right. This town doesn't need people like him. Anyways, eat up, kids!"

"Thanks a lot, Betty." Jake said as the plump waitress walked back to the kitchen.

Jake and the rest was about to start eating when something had caught his mind, and decided to ask Betty something.

"Where do you live again, Betty?" he called out to the waitress.

"177 Springfield Street" she replied.

That street name was familiar. Springfield Street was where Karen's house was located, and the number on her house was 178. Karen had lived next door to Betty's and the only tree that would be found on that street was next to the sidewalk between the two houses. The branches were thick and stretched out toward the the green hedge that separated them.

Alan was familiar with that street name and number as well, so he too called out a question to Betty. "And when did you noticed Peterson was spying on you?"

"Think it was...last Friday night." she replied back.

Alan, Alice, and Jake's eyes widened. Alan remembered that night when he got a call from Karen's parents saying she had been missing. Her parents heard a scream and when they went upstairs to the bedroom, she was no where to be found and the black print was shown on the floor. If Old Man Peterson was up on that tree, that night, then he may have been the last person who've seen Karen around the same time she vanished.

"Looks like I'm gonna have to talk to Old Man Peterson and find out what to do with him after lunch." Alan said, stuffing face with hamburgers.

"Well, I'm gonna go to see Pastor Brian later on and see if he needs any help with preparations for the funeral." Alice told everyone at the table as she began munching on the fries.

"My aunt wants me to buy some stuff at the Food Market." Jake said filling his stomach with the mixture of fries, gravy and mozzarella cheese. "We may have some visitors after the funeral."

They all ate their lunch and each tipped Betty for the service. After they left the diner satisfied with their meal, they each went to their respective locations, Jake at the market, Alan back at the station, and Alice had gone to the church to see Pastor Brian. The last time she saw him was during that same night, when Alan received the call about Karen. When she looked around, there was no sign of the priest but heard a faint mumbling sound from one of the confessional booths. When she entered one, on the other side of the small, rectangular see-through screen, was Pastor Brian praying with eyes closed as if he was under some sort of meditation. He had suddenly snapped out of it when Alice spoke silently through the screen, nearly made his heart jumped. He had a disappointed look on his face when she did that but had quickly smiled for when he noticed the beautiful brunette sitting on the other side with her elegant smile.

The church located just three blocks from Alice's house had an exquisite exterior. The gray bricks that stretched from the back up toward the varnished front doors had showed the building's prolonged existence since the early 1920's. The white concrete had spanned from above the doorway up toward the steeple, surrounding a large circular stained window with a golden crucifix in which can be seen clearly at night by indoor lights. And the church's bell can be plainly seen from any distance, as well as the iron crucifix edged at the very top of the steeple. The exterior was beautiful enough but not as nearly as the interior when Alice walked in through the varnished, wooden doors.

The church was huge and was filled with the feeling of calm and peacefulness, as if God had welcomed Alice in His very own house. Walls were made of white concrete, ceramic tiles and plaster as carving of exquisite designs had brought the church to life. Rows and rows of benches were polished without a single spec dust on them, wooden pictures were hung on the walls, on both sides of the building depicting the life of Christ from his birth to his death and resurrection. An altar with rows of colourful, votive candles were seen at the right corner, after the last row of benches surrounding the a statue of Christ in his divine white and red robe. At the heart of the church was a white, concrete altar covered in white cloth with a golden crucifix draping over the middle facing the benches. Behind that altar was an old priest in his robe, praying with his eyes closed, silently, and faithfully as he had his golden goblet sitting on the altar next to him.

As Alice walked closer to the altar, she looked above the priest and glanced at large, golden crucifix big enough for people attending mass to clearly see. The significant size and quality of it had made her doing the sign of the cross instantly and did a quick prayer to God from her heart. When Pastor Mayne had finished his, he opened his eyes and saw the young brunette standing at the bottom of the steps glancing at the crucifix above and behind him.

"Alice, my child." the old priest said. His voice barely echoed in the church as if he just woke up from a deep sleep.

Alice already finished her prayer before he spoke. "Afternoon, Pastor Mayne. I just came to see if you need any help for the funeral tonight."

Pastor Mayne had admired her kind smile and warm spirit. He felt as if the heavens had given him a guardian angel and her voice had always calmed his soul.

"Oh, I think I'll be fine, child. I'm just doing a bit of rehearsing." Pastor Brian took the golden goblet and placed in the small, sacred cabinet located directly behind him. "It is such a tragedy for a kind angel like Karen to be taken away from us at a very young age."

"Yeah, it is. I mean who would do such a thing to her? Karen was loved by everyone including her peers. It's very doubtful that she had some enemies around town."

After he locked the sacred cabinet, Pastor Brian's left index finger raised up in terms of correction.

"Ah, many of us have enemies, Alice." he corrected her. "It's just that either they are smart enough not to show themselves or we are too blind to even notice them. And what about the other girl? Carol, her name was?"

"Yes, Carol Graham. Karen's best friend."

"Oh, another one so young. I am sure that she is safe and will return."

"I sure hope so. We just don't want another funeral like this one."

"Just have faith, my child. Just have faith."

Alice nodded at the pastor's words. Her eyes had suddenly caught attention to what was around his neck. She knew at first that he would be wearing a necklace with a small wooden crucifix of Christ, but she did not noticed the circular object behind it, made of gold with four small jewels etched on each spacial corner of the cross. The crucifix appeared as if it was attached to the circular object, possibly glued, taped or used some string.

"You know, thats kind of rare to see a priest wearing that kind of jewelry." Alice said as she help Pastor Brian folding up the drape.

"Oh this?" he said, glancing at the object around his neck. "This was given to me by my father when I was a little boy. He was the archaeologist who found the Black Cave at the campgrounds."

"Really?"

"Yes, he found this medallion deep in the cave and gave it to me on my twelfth birthday. After he disappeared a year after, probably got trapped in another excavation site filled with booby traps, I kept it with me as a memento to him all this time."

"And you have your cross attached to it?"

Pastor Brian laughed briefly.

"Yes, I would like to think that this medallion is also some kind of good-luck charm, or some sort of faith amplifier. When I pray to God, at the same time I pray to my father who is now with him."

"That's good to hear, Pastor Brian." Alice said feeling admiration to the early-seventies servant of God and his strong dedication to serve under Him.

Meanwhile at the police station, Alan was at his desk located not far from Sheriff Barkley's. He was going through certain files and doing the usual paperwork until Barkley walked by him.

"I don't know what to do with Old Man Peterson." he said following with a heavy sigh. "We're not sure if he's gonna be behaving like that again."

"Betty Schultz said he saw him during that night, when we got the call about Karen Hannah." Alan said to his superior. "He may have been the last person seeing her."

"Could be. Her parents told us that she arrived home that night from Carol's place and seemed a bit upset about something. Then they heard a scream from her bedroom, went upstairs and she was gone, only leaving that black body print. And Old Man Peterson was up on that tree spying on Betty Schultz. He heard the scream which startled him, making him fall off that tree and crashed on his bike."

"Are you sure that's what he told you?"

"I don't know. Now he's causing a ruckus saying the world will be eaten by darkness, or some other kind of bullshit."

"So do you think we should keep him in his cell a little longer?"

Barkley looked back in the cell hallway and noticed a little old man sitting quietly in his jail cell, barely visible in the light that only illuminated half of the hall.

"Yeah," he officially said. "Probably for another day or two."

At the same time, Jake was looking around the poultry section at the food market with the small list that his Aunt Laura had written for him. It wasn't much but some chicken legs, a twelve-pack of sodas and some cauliflower. Just when he was about to grab the package of chicken legs, he felt a cold breeze swiftly and barely touching his back. He would have thought it was just the breeze from the outdoors that came right in when people walked in and out of the market. But that cold feeling was different. It felt eerie, abnormal, out of place and Jake's body nearly shook by the effects of it. He looked behind him to see if anybody had passed by or someone playing a trick on him. There was nothing, just rows of canned goods and a barely visible shadow of himself, slightly covering a portion of the rows with its own darkness. Still, there was nothing. Whatever that was, it made Jake feel a bit uneasy.

The summer sun had begun to set and stars were partly visible through the dimmed sky. People from all over town, teachers, students, families, officials had gathered at the Greensburg Memorial Park to say their final goodbyes to the beloved Karen Hannah. The brown varnished coffin was sitting on a pair of leather straps, attached to some lowering mechanism. A large bouquet of multi-coloured flowers laid on top of the lid with several roses placed in front if it. A large photo stand with a cropped up picture of Karen, which was used as her graduation photo and to be placed on a plaque with others to be hung up in the cafeteria among others who graduated before them. There was no gravestone made yet, but Pastor Brian told her family it will be placed by the end of the month.

Jake stood in the crowd listening to Pastor Brian's speech about how that death was not really an end, but a beginning of another life. He even spoke of reincarnation and how that the resurrection of Christ can also happen to all mankind. It was all too familiar to Jake and his aunt Laura, as it reminded them about his parent's funeral. With his father's, people from the Carlton City Police Department attended the funeral at Greensburg. His mother wanted her husband to be buried in the same town as they lived, so they can be closer together in spirit. When little six-year-old Jake stood and listen to the priest's words and prayers, he watched other members of the police force, dressed in their formal uniforms with their rifles in hand. And when the speech and prayers had stopped, the neatly dressed police officers aimed their rifles at the sun above and fired three rounds. The rifles echoed, tearing through the silence that bestowed upon the people at the cemetery. Every time they roared, Jake nearly jumped and barely shook in between each shot. He was thinking if it was those same shots that killed his father, loud and painful. The last shot nearly scared him and clutched onto his mother with tears in his eyes. When it was over, both him and his mother approached the coffin and said one last goodbye to a good husband and a wonderful father until the lowering mechanism had turned on and brought the coffin into the opened ground.

The funeral was over and Karen's coffin began to lower into the ground. Her parents had said their final goodbyes as Carol Graham's family held on to their tears for their daughter. Jake looked around and through the townspeople who attended the funeral and saw everyone there. Sheriff Barkley, the town's Mayor, Principal Dale Winston, the rest of the faculty, deputy Alan next to Barkley, Alice was on Jake's right side and his aunt Laura and cousin Becky on his left. But Jake had a feeling someone else was missing, so he whispered Alice something in her ear.

"Wasn't Jason supposed to be here?" he asked.

Alice shook her head with disappointment for her boyfriend to not show up.

"Just got a call from him while I with Pastor Brian." she whispered back. "He was coming back from the city when he hit a moose. He said that the impact had caused the engine to stall and wouldn't start. Now he had to have it towed all the way home"

Jake remembered that Jason had driven a pick-up, but it belonged to his father who happened to be a strict farmer. And to hear what Alice said, Jason's father would go up in flames and roar at him.

"Wow," Jake said with a slight laugh. "His dad's not gonna like that."

"I'm gonna go talk to Karen's parents for a minute." Alice said.

"Sure."

Alice disappeared between the townsfolk and walked up to Karen's family who were talking to Carol Graham's and Pastor Brian. Jake took another look at his surroundings and other gravestones around the cemetery until he spotted one that he recognized. Five rows behind Karen's was a large, marbled headstone big enough for two graves. Flowers were placed on both on top of the stone as well as on the base along side a police badge. It was the graves of Jake's parents. He walked up to it and read the entire graving on the stone and quietly begun to pray to them.

Jake knelt down and turned his eyes on his father's name, 'Detective Jeremy Miller' and began to speak to him from his sad heart.

"Hey, Dad," he said quietly "It's me. Looks like I've lost a friend today. And another one had disappeared, possibly by the same person who killed Karen. If I was detective like you, I would have find that out myself. But seeing you lying here had changed my mind of becoming one. I'm pretty sure you wanted me to follow you in your footsteps, but decided not too. All the stories you told me about detectives and how they solved crimes were pretty inspiring, but not as wonderful as reality itself. And that reality is why your lying here next to Mom. Being a member of the police force may be something worth doing, something to make a difference in your life as well as others. But I realized that it's also dangerous, especially if your stationed in a corrupt like Carlton City. I miss you so much, dad."

Jake then turned his eyes toward his mother's name, 'Olivia Miller' and spoke to her the same way.

"Hey, Mom. As you can see out there, I've lost a friend today. But I guess you heard it all already. One thing I do not understand is why would take your own life like that. Why did you leave me alone so quickly? I can't remember much but I know you had some deep depression but I've known you long enough that you wouldn't do that to yourself. You've never left a note, not a single word. Why, Mom?

What made you do that? Was it because of Dad? Was it because of the people at work? Was it me?"

Jake shook his head trying to remember what happened before his mother hung herself. It felt like there was a giant hole in his past that had been taken away. He only remembered his mother smiling at him saying that everything will be alright after losing her job at the diner. But it was all blank after that.

"Well, whatever it was," Jake continued as tears began to fall on his cheeks, "I miss you so much."

"You okay, Jake?" Alice appeared next to him.

Jake looked up and quickly wiped away the tears.

"Yeah, just talking to Mom and Dad."

"Well, I talked to Karen's parents and they gave me this."

Alice showed Jake a small, pink-coloured book with flowers drawn on it and a strap with a small lock to seal it's pages. It was Karen's diary.

"They wanted you to keep that?" Jake asked.

"Well, they had no idea who to give it to, but since I happened to a close friend to both Karen and Carol, they wanted me to keep it as a memento. They haven't looked into the diary themselves, figured that some secrets are best kept with her."

"But don't you think it's a good idea to have a look? I mean there must have something she had written that may gave us a clue of what happened."

"I'll look into it later. This is girl stuff, after all." she said glaring down at Jake's eyes with somewhat serious but teasing look. She thought she would let him or Alan look into Karen's private entries. But Jake had already understood what Alice had said. Even after graduation, they were still teenage girls at heart.

Night had suddenly fallen and everyone was already at their homes, either sleeping, reading, or watching TV. Jake was up in bedroom sitting at his desk with his pencil moving swiftly and fluidly. When he was in the seventh grade, his English teacher introduced the class, 'The Writing Process.' Basically it was to teach students how novels were made before they ended up on their shelves. They come up with a story idea, write it down on paper, review it to their classmates to see if there is any improvements or more ideas to add on to, re-write with what they acquired, get it edited by the teacher, do a final copy and get graded on it. Jake was fascinated by it and when he first wrote a story about a kid detective solving the case of the stolen lunch box, he did others like it and the teacher gave him a row of grades between 'B-' to 'A+.' What he was writing at his desk that night was basically notes for locations, settings and character information. Another detective story was on Jake's mind but sometimes his imagination was interrupted by memories of his father. He would stopped writing and g at the picture frame that was sat in the corner of his desk. The same family picture that his aunt Laura had taken when his father had visited his family for the weekend for the first time. At first he wasn't sure about writing more detective stories after his father died but with all the good stories he told him, Jake took the inspiration and began to write them down.

Jake was about to continue writing until he felt the same, cool breeze blowing on his back, similar to what he felt at the food market. Except it was more colder and more eerie before. He thought it came from the door behind him so he looked back to check if it was opened. It wasn't, the door was closed and all he could see was the warm light from his desk lamp flooding only a quarter of his room and his own shadow stretching from the legs of his chair all the way to the bottom edge of the door from where his head would barely touch. He thought it was just his imagination so he turned back to his writing.

The breeze came again, colder like as if winter had fallen in his bedroom. He looked at the window and noticed it was shut. He had already closed it when he arrived home from the funeral, so there was no indication a cold breeze like that would enter, so he turned his head at the door behind him again. That's strange, he thought. When he first saw his shadow, it had stretched just to the bottom of the door but it seemed to be stretching more and his torso would show at the middle, parallel to the doorknob. He checked his desk lamp to see if it had moved or so, but it was nailed down to his desk. There was no way the lamp would be moved, not even the head of the lamp.

Jake begun to shiver, not because of the cold breeze but he felt as if something was happening around him. He tried to think that he may be overdoing it and fatigue had already settled in, making him seeing things that only people with vivid imagination would see. He rubbed his eyes and tried to breathe just to calm him down. But when he let out his breath, it made a mist. A white mist had flew out of his mouth, mixing the hot carbon dioxide with cold air he was breathing. Not only that, his body felt colder and colder as if his entire room had turned into a giant freezer. He suddenly felt as if someone was standing behind him, creeping on him, ready to pounce of his life as he sat there vulnerable and both quivering with fear and shivering with the piercing cold. He slowly turned his eyes toward what was behind him and after what he saw, he jumped out of his chair and something had quickly wrapped around his throat.

Jake's shadow was enormous and even darker. The silhouette that shaped his figure had its grasp around his throat, nearly choking him. The grasp was ice cold, nearly like dry ice and it was pulling Jake toward its own dark void. As Jake was being pulled closer to his monstrous shadow, the black surface became solid, then warped like puddle of black oil. Trying to pry his shadow's cold hands, he suddenly saw something slowly emerging from the black pool. It was all dark and it appeared to have long hair, with eyes burning bright yellow. As it emerged even more, a face of a woman was revealed and even with its dark, oily appearance, Jake had recognized the woman's face instantly.

It was Jake's mother that emerged from the black, oily pool of his shadow's chest. Crying out and screaming at him like a whaling, tortured ghost.

"I'm sorry!" the dark face cried out to him. *"I'M SORRY!"*

Jake was terrified to see his mother in that state. He would scream but his shadow's tightening grip wouldn't allow him. After hearing his mother's warped and distorted voice, her hands suddenly emerged from the pool, aiming for her son to grab him bring him closer to the black pool. He his nose had barely touched the pool and it felt cold, as cold as death. If he would die this way, at least he would be with his Mom and Dad very soon.

But that opportunity had been taken away when the door of his bedroom open and the ceiling lights went on. The black shadow had suddenly disappeared, the cold was instantly gone, back to its room temperature, and Jake fell to the floor gasping for air with black, oily stains around his neck. It was his Aunt Laura that saved him. After seeing her nephew shaking, coughing and choking on the floor, she quickly went up to him.

"Oh, my God, Jake." she said. "What happened?"

Jake tried to speak to her about what just happened, but after seeing all that, something had sparked in his mind and only said one thing.

"What the fuck was that?"

Chapter 5

Jake could not sleep after what happened. He was still shaken by the whole thing that occurred in his bedroom, but what he could not get his mind off was the fact the Old Man Peterson was there when Karen Hannah had vanished and killed. He may have been too busy being a peeping tom, spying on Betty Schultz who lived next door to Karen's, but Jake was sure that the old man must have seen something. So, after a quick breakfast, we briskly walked out of the house and was heading toward the police station to where Old Man Peterson was held. The sun was still rising and sky was still clear, but Jake did not stop to admire the weather. He wanted answers. He wanted to know what was that thing that attacked him and want to figure out if it was that same thing that attacked Karen and snatched Carol Graham during the graduation.

While he was getting closer to station, he suddenly saw Alan getting into his patrol vehicle and drove off, assuming he was heading toward the Greensburg's campgrounds. He wanted to check to see if he can talk to Old Man Peterson, but when he saw his best friend disappeared into the woods, his only chance was to talk to the town sheriff Clarence Barkley. What he did not realized was that Alice Craig was also at the station, as Jake walked through the main doors.

Alice saw Jake walked in but noticed his eyes were baggy, almost red and a bit shaken, as if he hadn't slept at all.

"Jake, are okay?" Alice said, but Jake ignored her and went straight to Sheriff's desk to where he sat.

"You still have Old Man Peterson locked up here?" Jake asked firmly.

"Why, yes." Barkley said, nearly startled by Jake's sudden presence. "He's.."

Barkley was about to point his thumb toward the cell hall but Jake already knew where it was. His sudden turn and brisk walk with a thirst for answers had cut Barkley's words and saw the old man sitting on his bed in his cell, quiet as a mouse and looking down on the filthy, concrete floor.

"Mister Peterson?" Jake called out almost echoing the jail cell.

The old man's bald head raised and his small, sunken eyes looked directly through the bars.

"Yeah," the old man said calmly, "that's me."

"You were at Springfield Street, on that tree spying on Betty that night."

Old Man Peterson slowly got up from the bed but very slowly due to the injury he had gotten from falling off that same tree.

"Yeah, I was looking at the pretty piece of ham."

Assuming that he was still be drunk, his attitude and manners were non-existent from this seventy-one-year-old man.

"Did you see anything from the house, next door to Betty's?"

The old man walked up toward the bars staring into nothing, but slowly gave the expression that he knew what Jake was talking about.

"Ah, yes. The little Hannah girl." then his expression faded and his eyebrows lowered. "Why should I tell you? You wouldn't believe me, anyways."

Jake stretched the collar of his shirt revealing bruised markings around his neck, left by that shadowy figure that attacked him, last night.

"Because who or what attacked Karen, almost got me as well."

Alice walked up to Jake and saw the markings.

"Jesus, Jake." she exclaimed. "What happened to you?"

Jake ignored her again.

"Tell me what you saw." Jake repeated with more effort and more clearly.

There was a pause, then Old Man Peterson had finally gave him what he knew.

"Yeah," he said. "I was on that tree. I heard that Betty was gonna go to the movies with her husband that night, so I figured that I might get a free show. I've seen her through her window many times. Sometimes she would caught me, but I never stop. I drove my bike there and went up with my binoculars to have closer look. I tell ya, that Betty's got a nice plump figure. It makes me feel fifty-years younger."

He started laughing but was interrupted by loud coughs due to his aged lungs.

"Anyways, I was sitting up on that branch, having a free peep show when I saw a light turned on through the upstairs window, next door. I took a small peek through there with my binoculars and there was the little Hannah girl, sitting at her desk."

"And then what?" Jake asked.

"She looked as if she was crying or something. Like as if she either lost something or did something wrong, I don't know. It wasn't my business so I turned my binoculars back at Betty. And I tell ya, that Betty Schultz has the biggest ham hocks that she would need two guys to be her new support bra."

Peterson laughed again. The insults and jokes were enough to offend Jake, maybe offend Alice even more.

Jake wanted Peterson to stop and get on with his story but he was to willing to hear what other things that Peterson had seen.

"And when I was about to...well you know... relieve some tension in my pants when I heard a scream. It came from that window next door. I looked back to where the Hannah girl was, and holy shit!"

"What was it?" Jake asked with his eyes widened with some suspense.

"I don't know what it was, but something flew out from behind her! It was like a giant, black arm or some muscular dude wearing black. Then I saw the little hands coming out of this dude's chest! Little, black girly hands grabbing on her. The next thing you know, she was pulled down to the floor! Seeing that happening, I was thinking of trying to save her life. I tried to get down from the tree to help her but I slipped off and fell on my fucking bike!"

Jake began to clarify his story and tried compare it to what had happened to him last night. Whatever grabbed Karen and Carol could have been what Jake had seen, but it was hard for him to picture something like that from Peterson's point of view.

"If you say that whatever attacked her did the same to you," Peterson added on, "you were lucky that you didn't end up like her, six feet under and no birthday suit."

Alice shook her head, still could not figure out what was going on.

"I don't know what this is all about, Jake." Alice said. "And where did you get those marks on your neck?"

"Would you believe me that it was my own shadow that did this?" Jake whispered to Alice.

"I would think that your nuts."

"Then we're gonna have to go check the stage at the gymnasium, and maybe Karen's bedroom."

"Hey, wait a second there, sonny." Old Man Peterson called out to Jake. "Your face kind of reminded me of someone I know."

He took a closer look at his young face and his features had sparked his memory of seeing someone who used to work at the tavern near the outside edge of town.

"Yeah, that's right. You reminded me of that sweet girl who worked at the bar a long time ago. Olivia, was it?"

Jake paused for a bit. He did remember his mother used to be a bartender at the town's local tavern when he was six. But the rest was all fuzzy to him. All he can remember was his mother working at the diner at day time, and at the bar at night.

"Yeah," Jake softly spoke.

"She was the most beautiful girl I've met. Sexy figure, glowing face, sparkling eyes, the works. She even had a nice pair on her chest too."

Peterson winked with a laugh.

Jake felt a surge of anger in him, letting this old man talking about his mother like that. His loosen hands had slowly turned into hard fists, fingers tucked tightly under fearing or an incoming impact.

"I heard she hung herself after she quit." The old man then shrugged. "All I wanted from her was a piece of that fine ass."

Anger had grew even more in Jake's body, filling him with thoughts of beating Peterson right down the filthy concrete from where he stood.

"You better shut the fuck up!" Jake bluntly said but nearly shouted. "That girl happened to be my mother. So you better show some respect, old man."

Peterson's expression went from a happy pervert to a sudden shock and then slowly sank into remorse.

"Oh, I'm sorry about that." he said. "It's a shame, really. Cause if your mother hadn't hung herself..." but it turned out that the remorse was just a ruse, a fake expression. "...I could have been your new dad."

Peterson's perverted smile came back with a laugh and another wink. But that face didn't last long as one of Jake's fists flew right through the bars and right into his crooked teeth. Peterson flew back a few feet, landed on his side while Jake had clutched his fist feeling a slight tearing pain. The impact had tore a muscle in his wrist, spraining it.

"Jake!" Alice cried out, trying to hold him back. "Calm down. Take it easy."

"You rotten piece of expired shit!" Jake spat at the fallen old man. "I hope you rot in your fucking cell!"

Sheriff Barkley heard the commotion and directed Jake away from the cell. He then turned toward Peterson, struggling to get up on the filthy bed.

"Now, you just sit there and keep that mouth shut, ya hear?"

"I'm sorry you had to hear all that, Jake." Alice said giving some comfort to her friend. "Did you hurt yourself?"

"I'll be fine." Jake replied. "But I really need to take a look at the stage floor at the school's gymnasium."

"That wouldn't be possible." Sheriff Barkley heard their conversation. "That stage is now a crime scene and so does Karen's bedroom. No civilian is allowed on those premises."

"Please, Sheriff Barkley just..."

"I said no!" Barkley's barking voice stopped Jake in his tracks. "Listen, Jake. I know your trying to follow your father's footsteps and he and I go way back. But it takes proper training to become one, or you could at least become just a regular police officer. But until then, you don't go to the school nor the girl's bedroom until this whole thing is resolved."

"Yes, sir." Jake said with a slight nod.

"The last thing I want is a bunch of kids meddling with police business. Now if you excuse me, I got some paper work to fill out."

Sheriff Barkley walked back to his desk as Alice and Jake began to walk out of the police station. Jake's idea had never changed, even after hearing the barking orders of his father's former partner.

"Looks like we'll have to wait till nightfall." Jake said to himself.

"Are you crazy?" Alice said, thinking about the outcome of doing what Jake was thinking. "We can get in big trouble, and I do mean arrested."

Jake turned his serious eyes to Alice's.

"Do you really think the police would believe that a giant, black monster killed Karen, kidnapped Carol and nearly devoured me? I just want proof."

"What proof?"

"Whatever attacked me last night, could be that same thing that gotten our fellow classmates."

Jake's mind suddenly sparked, missing out something obvious.

"By the way," Jake said with a puzzled look to Alice, "why are you here?"

"I was gonna talk to Alan about something, but he had to leave. He said he got a call from a family up at the campgrounds that their two-year-old son went missing in the woods."

Jake noticed Alice was holding Karen Hannah's diary, but the strap seemed to be detached. The diary was unlocked.

"Did you find something in that diary?" Jake asked, pointed out the little pink booklet.

"That's what I want Alan to check out. Read Karen's last entry."

Alice handed Jake the diary and opened it. He flipped through the pages, looking through the dates until he found one entry she wrote on the night she was reported missing.

June 12th, 2009

Dear, Diary

I've finished writing my valedictory speech for my graduation from Greensburg High School. It was very difficult for me to do, since three-quarters of it is basically my confession. My confession to all the families, teachers, and friends. I had a fight with Carol, today. She wanted me to keep doing what I have been doing all these years but I told her that I decided to tell everyone the truth. She didn't want all that hard work we had done go to waste, and she said if I fall, she won't fall with me. I understood her decision, but after what we had done, I don't deserve to be an honourable student. I don't deserve to be valedictorian. I don't deserve to earn a diploma, getting that recommendation from Doctor Cummings, even though our session we had was just a certain fling. I don't even deserve to be psychiatrist. I deserve to be locked up in jail, I deserve to be expelled, repeat school all over again, I deserve to be punished and I will pay up for my sins. I haven't told my parents yet, but when the day comes, they will know. I'm sorry, Carol. You've been my best friend since forever, but I have to do this.

Jake could not believe what he had read. The fact that a kind, loving person such as Karen would hide something that may cost everything she had worked so hard for. And that line of text about Doctor Cummings, ' *even though our session we had was just a certain fling,*' had puzzled Jake even more. Could it be that Karen had an affair with Doctor Cummings just so she can get the recommendation? Jake shook his head, trying not to believe that.

"We got to take a look at that speech she written." Jake said, reading the entry again but at even quicker pace.

"It's locked up tight in the evidence room." Alice said. "We'll have to wait until Alan gets back."

"Well, I'm not gonna let and old man with a badge stopping me from even taking a peek at the stage, tonight. My dad used to tell me that sometimes, in order to find the truth you have to risk everything. And that includes your job and your life. In this case, our lives and our freedom."

"I'm not going with you." Alice said, backing away from Jake. She wasn't ready to risk the opportunity to lose her goal of becoming a fashion designer just so she would go on a wild goose chase.

"Please, Alice." Jake said, almost begging. "I may need your help with this. We'll just be there around midnight. The cops won't see us."

There was a pause and Alice got confused. At first, she did not wanted more of her friends ended up like Karen, or being kidnapped like Carol. And at the same time, she wanted to know the truth about what was happening but when she saw Jake's bruises around his neck and what Old Man Peterson told him, she lost control of her thoughts and went with her instinct.

"Okay," Alice finally spoke with a heavy sigh. "But you owe me an acceptance to the University." Then, Alice noticed that Jake was still clutching as his hand, the one he used on Peterson. "You should have that checked."

Jake nodded. That day was a good idea to do so, since his cousin Becky wanted to see her fellow classmate at the hospital, Amanda Riley. She was diagnosed with a rare disease which cause her heart to weaken. Day by day, her heart slowly began beat slower and a bit quieter and she felt weaker every week that passed by. She and Becky were best friends since kindergarten and she was hit by that illness about a month before Karen was found dead. Becky would visit her every weekend to cheer her up, and every time she saw her, it would seem that the freckles on that little blond face were fading, one by one. Her complexion had become paler and paler and she felt sleepy and more sleepy as if her life was slowly fading away.

Jake's family doctor, Dr. Marcus Chandler had began to wrap around Jake's injured hand with a silk bandage.

"You should take it easy with that." the doctor ordered. "But don't worry about it. Almost everyone in town wanted to take a swing at Old Man Peterson."

Jake slowly nodded with a light smile, assuming that he may not have been the first. "He just needs to watch what he was saying." he said, "especially about Mom."

Doctor Chandler was the same doctor who treated Jake's post-traumatic stress that he suffered after seeing his mother's dead body hanging in her bedroom. He was able to cope with it but he could not forget the fact that he lost both his parents, and within a short period of time between each death. He felt so alone, like an ordinary orphan lost in the world with no one to love, no one to hold his hand, and no one to help him grow up to be a better man. That was when his aunt, Laura Chambers, younger sister of his mother, Olivia, decided to take him under her wing. She was the only family little Jake had, since his grandfather had died of a stroke and his grandmother passed away due to lung cancer, both on his mother's side. Jake never had a father-figure nor a big-brother during his stay with his aunt but with her as being some sort of tomboy, it sure made up for the missing male companion.

"Still can't remember anything, Jake?" Doctor Chandler asked.

Jake shook his head.

"No," he told him. "It's still blank, in there."

"I'm pretty sure whatever memory you lost will show up eventually. But some people are better off without them. The only thing is, you remembered seeing your mother's dead body but you can't remember anything before.

Jake sighed again.

"Yeah."

There was a huge gap between the last time his mother smiled at him and the night he got out of bed and found her suspended body in her bedroom. The last time she smiled was about two weeks after his father's funeral. Even though depression had already began to settle upon her soul, she tried to stay positive and told her six-year-old son that everything will be fine. That was about as far as he can remember, but it felt like somebody had cut out a big scene from his life, like a rejected portion of a Hollywood film and placed it somewhere in storage in case the they release it on DVD as either bonus material or a director's cut. He tried so hard to remember but there was nothing but pure darkness. He felt there was something important hiding in that dark, blank, forgotten memory. Something he may have seen, heard, said or felt. But whatever it was, it was way out of his reach.

"But whatever it is," Jake said, "It felt like I'm missing something important."

"Well," Doctor Chandler said, also with a sigh, "I would suggest not letting it get to your head. You are happy with what you have now, are you?"

Jake smiled, realizing he still had Aunt Laura and little Becky to give him all the support that he needed.

"Yeah." Jake said. "Aunt Laura and Becky were both helpful. You know what? Maybe I should concentrate on what's ahead of me then being swallowed by my own pain."

"That's the spirit, Jake." Doctor Chandler said, feeling a bit proud of his patient. "Well, let me write you a prescription for some gel that would help with the muscles in your hand."

"Thanks."

While Doctor Chandler began to write Jake's prescription, he turned his attention to a nearby room located in the recovery wing. The door was wide opened enough to reveal where Aunt Laura and Becky was and who was lying in that hospital bed wearing an oxygen mask. It was Becky's classmate and best friend, Amanda Riley. Weak and sleepy by her illness, the eight-year-old blond girl with freckles barely visible due to her pale complexion, was speaking slowly and quietly to her best friend standing at her bedside. Becky stood there, while almost made a tear, listened the dying girl's words.

That heart breaking scenery had reminded Jake of his grandmother, who passed away from lung cancer. The elegant lady, lying in the hospital bed with the oxygen mask, was only able to whisper as she continuously losing strength in her one lung while the other was already dead. She was fading fast but the doctors had given her drugs to ease her breathing muscles from any pain and made her breathe her remaining oxygen more naturally. And when the time came, her last breath escaped from her body, as well as her spirit. Every family member who witnessed her passing that night, had said goodbye from the bottom of their hearts and wished her happiness and joy in Heaven. That may happen again with Amanda.

"How is she?" Jake asked his doctor, referring to the sick and dying child.

Doctor Chandler looked up from Jake's prescription file toward Amanda, with a sad expression on his face.

"She's stable, as of now." he concluded. "But she's fading fast."

"Is there a way she can be saved?"

"There is a way." Chandler took off his reading glasses. "The big heads at the Carlton City Hospital is willing to perform special surgery that may save her, but..."

After Jake heard that, he quickly turned his head back at his doctor, assuming what he was about to say next may not be good news.

"But, what?" Jake asked concernedly.

"The cost of the surgery is very high, even beyond our price range. Her parents had already sold their farm, both living in a small apartment in the city. They are both working two jobs each to earn enough money for the surgery. But with employment rate at a all time low due to the accelerated crime rate thats happening over there, they were only able to pay three-quarters of it. All they need was another ten-thousand dollars to cover the expense. And with Amanda's condition deteriorating fast, she may not be able to live through her ninth birthday, next week."

Jake's heart felt like crumbling into small pieces when Doctor Chandler told him all that. But Becky would feel even worse if Amanda would give up and let her innocent soul disappear from that weak shell. They would not converse with each other, laugh with each other, play with each other, smile at each other. Becky did not want to lose a friend like that. Every time she and her mom arrived home from visiting Amanda, she would walk up the stairs, into her bedroom and cry herself silently to sleep. Those two were inseparable, best of friends since the beginning. Her childhood life would change instantly and the pain of losing a good friend like that would burn her throughout her teenage and adult years. Jake had wished he could do something to help, but there are certain things that you cannot change. Sometimes you can try to do your hardest to help out someone in need, but sometimes they became in vain. He told Becky that as long as she kept memories of Amanda alive within her, she will never be lost. And the best way was to keep the bracelet that Amanda had made her during Art class, which signified true friendship.

Both Becky and Amanda each a wore a hand-made bracelet and had not took them off since. Amanda had hers still wrapped around her wrist, barely showing underneath the bedsheets, rainbow coloured with flowers and hearts. Becky's bracelet was made of stretched cotton balls and small black beads with ears that formed little rabbits. Becky believed that the rabbit was her spiritual animal and she adores them when she and her mom visited Amanda's farm filled with baby chicks, and rabbits frolicking around behind the fence. She had missed those times when Amanda was lively and full of energy. But her parents had to sell their farm just to pay off a large portion of their daughter's upcoming surgery, but i wasn't enough.

"Let's hope to God, if there's some kind of miracle to save that poor child." Doctor murmured to himself.

Jake was hoping too, not just for Amanda's sake, but also for Becky's and the bond that they shared together.

"Hang on tight, Amanda." Jake whispered to himself.

Chapter 6

Alice walked up to her boyfriend's garage where he was seen with his head underneath the opened hood of his father's pick-up. When Jason told his old man about it, his father flamed. He was not gonna pay up money to get it repaired so he got his son to do the entire fix-up. The front end of the pick-up was pretty damaged. The right headlight was busted, the front bumper was missing, the windshield was cracked all the way across and the radiator along with the frontal frame was bent inward, like as if it ran into a tree.

"Jesus, Jason." Alice exclaimed, seeing the damage. "Your just lucky your not hurt."

"Yeah," Jason Baker said to his girlfriend with a light sigh. "But my dad didn't thought about it that way."

His father was mad as hell when heard about it. He was known to be making pointless assumptions and mindless conclusions. When Jason told his about it, he thought if son may had been drinking on the back home after he got word from the football coach at Carlton City would accept him to try-out for the team. He just wanted excellence from his son, not excuses, no failures, no mishaps. Results, accomplishment and pure proficiency was what he wanted out of him. And having his own son damage his pick-up was completely unacceptable.

"Are you sure you hit a moose?" Alice asked, just be sure.

"Y-yeah," Jason replied with a little stutter in his voice. "I think it was the ass end of it. The moose was able to crawl back into the woods, but..."

His sentence was cut short. He had a bit of a hard time trying to explain it all, but Alice thought he may be still a bit shaken by the accident. Then Jason changed the subject very quickly with one simple question.

"You want a beer?" he asked.

"Sure." Alice replied a kind expression.

For long as Alice new him, Jason had repeated grades when he was in elementary school, so it would be understandable for him to be drinking at his age. Jason was twenty years old, just one year past the legal drinking limit. But Alice was eighteen, one year below the legal age, but she did not care since her birthday would arrive two days before she would attend University at Carlton City.

As Jason went to get two cans of beer in the kitchen, inside the house, Alice began to inspect the damage of the pick-up a little closer. The damage on the front end was pretty bad, despite the impact was on the rump end of a wondering moose.

"Did you even see the moose?" Alice asked out to her boyfriend.

"No," he replied back from the kitchen. "I was on my way home until one just ran right across the road."

Alice kept looking around the pick-up, and took a g at the guts underneath the hood.

"What made the engine kick out, anyways?"

"I'm not sure. I first I thought the spark plug came loose, but it's still in there. Then I looked at all the belts, battery wires, alternators, and they seem fine."

Alice slowly walked to the driver side and looked inside the cab. The air bag didn't burst out, so it could mean that the impact wasn't that strong. Then she noticed something underneath the steering wheel. The column underneath was slightly ajar, as if someone had forced it open and tried to put it back in its place but failed.

Then Alice asked Jason a curious question while her boyfriend arrived with the two cans of beer.

"Have you tried hot wiring it?"

Jason shook his head.

"Nope. I never even thought of that. But even if I did, it may not work anyways."

Alice made a confused look.

"That's strange cause steering column is..."

Alice's cell phone rang from her jacket pocket. When she looked a the bright, blue LCD screen, it was blinking in large black words, 'Alan.' She answered the ringing cell phone as she took a small drink of the beer.

"Alan," she spoke in the cell phone. "What's up?"

"Hey, sis," Alan's voice rang out of the earphone. "Where you at?"

"I'm at Jason's. He's fixing his dad's pick-up."

"You know that last entry in Karen's diary that you showed to Barkley? He brought out that sheet of paper from the evidence room which it looked like the speech she wrote for the graduation. You better have a look at this."

"Alright, I'll be there soon. Bye."

Alice hung up her phone.

Jason took a huge gulp of his beer

"Got something about Karen there, babe?" Jason asked.

"Yeah," Alice replied. "I'm gonna head town to the station and see what my brother's got. I'll talk to you later, love."

"Alright. I'll call ya later, tonight."

"Bye, Jason."

Alice winked at her boyfriend when she walked out of the garage, showing some swings just to make Jason nearly choke on his own beer. But what she didn't realize that she was going to help Jake with entering the school and check out the stage at the gymnasium. Despite Jason's shortcomings, he and Alice were completely inseparable. Their eyes had never been pulled away by anything and their bond would last a life time, even more. They even promised each other not to keep secrets from each other. But when Alice walked out of Jason's garage, his heart began to beat faster and the thoughts of telling his girlfriend the truth ran through his mind. He wished what happened in the woods had never took place, and if he told the truth, it would jeopardize his chance of being a member of Carlton City's football team, and even worse, might end up prison.

Alice drank the last of the beer and threw it at a nearby recycling bin, down the street. The police station was not far from Jason's house, almost a ten minute walk. But with her feeling energetic   and the warm feeling of the weather, it almost took her half the time to reach the station.

She walked through the doors and saw Alan talking to Sheriff Barkley. As she was walking toward the sheriff's desk, she g at the ten 'Missing Child' that was the wall on her left. With small disappointed g, she felt as if the police had given up on finding the ten little girls that went missing. Since they have been gone for a long time, it would be easily assumed that they may be dead. But she never gave up hope. Dead or alive, she prayed for those little girls to arrive home.

"Hey Alice." Alan said as her sister approached him.

"Hi, Alan." she said. "What you got?"

In Alan's hand was a zipped-up plastic bag with a sheet of paper in it. On that paper was the valedictory speech that Karen Hannah had written for the graduation ceremony and the same one that Carol Graham was presenting before she disappeared.

"After I read what's on this paper," Alan said with a somewhat shocked look, "I'd nearly turned white."

Alan handed the evidence over and began reading what was on that piece of paper that Karen had written before she was killed.

"To Everyone who attended this memorable time, I would like to say that for past twelve years, we have never been more happy and proud to our teachers who taught us everything that exist in this world we live in. From the stories and fairy tales you read to the alphabets and numbers, from the history of our country and this town to the ways of how molecules and learning the periodic table, you all had show us the way and we are grateful for it. But that's not all. It's a big world, out there. And when the time comes when we are ready for what is ahead of us, we will continue on and strive for a better tomorrow"

Alice remembered hearing Carol Graham saying all that. Even though it was Karen Hannah who wrote it, her best friend had delivered it to the crowd and Karen would never been more proud of her. But her feeling of confidence was suddenly wipe out by what was following after that.

"On a final note, I would like to point out is what I have written here was very difficult for me because after twelve years I have been to this school, I had wished that I would start all over again. You may see me as a straight A student, intelligent, talented and seeing me as a

future psychiatrist, but to tell you the truth....the whole truth...I'm none of these things but a lying, cheating fraud.

Before I met my friend Carol Graham, I was struggling. I tried so hard to study and I could never have made it until she came in our school. She came to my side and asked that if she can help me. How she would help me made me think twice, but I've always wanted to be a psychiatrist and help people with their problems. But I was the one with problems. I accepted her offer but when she started altering report cards, copying off of a copyrighted material and slightly changed it to appear as if it was my own, lying to certain teachers about my success when they are really failures, I would have thought she may have done the same in her previous school.

But my dream of becoming a psychiatrist became first, so I went along with it. I even believed my own lies and cheats and even when so far as to have a psychiatric evaluation with my chemistry teacher, Doctor Cummings. And when I meant far, I meant it wasn't an evaluation. I've used my body to get him to give the recommendation for a scholarship and told him not to tell anyone about it.

When the time came to write this speech, my conscious had came to me and told me everything that I have done to progress this far. It didn't felt good. I felt like throwing up and crying forever. I have never felt so guilty in my life and I even told my friend Carol that I would tell everybody at the ceremony the truth.

So after all these years, I'm a liar, a cheater, and I have branded myself as the Class Fraud. I rather be in jail for what I have done all these years. And I will make up for it by repeating every grade and study the right way, not the coward way. I am sorry for you all, and I am sorry for the rest of the class and teachers. Please find a way to forgive me. Thank you.."

Alice froze after reading the entire speech. She would never have thought that one of her classmates had lied and cheated her way to be a honourable student of Greensburg High School. And what was even worse is that the session she had with the chemistry teacher was just a one night stand. Karen had sex with Doctor William Cummings just so she can get the recommendation and the scholarship to take the course of psychiatry at the University. It was too much for her to take in, too much that she lost her train of thought and was replaced by garbled images of Karen cheating and seducing teachers. And to think that

Carol had helped her do those things, she was pretty sure that she may have persuade her to do that, but still.

Alice shook her head in disbelief.

"This is..." she said. "This is unacceptable. I can't believe what I just read."

"We're gonna have a talk with Doctor Cummings." Alan suggested. "Besides, Karen was only sixteen when she was killed."

Alice nearly snapped out of the confusion and nodded at his brother.

"In the meantime," Sheriff Barkley barked, got off from his desk chair. "You should leave the rest of this to us. This is a police business, after all."

Alan just stood there when his superior decided to cut in between him and his sister. He was pretty strict about what he said and assumed what he would say next.

Alice agreed with the nod and walked out of the station. Barkley turned his piercing to his deputy with his finger pointed right as his face, looking mighty pissed.

"As for you, Craig," Barkley snapped, "you better keep your trap shut from spilling out our affairs here."

"But sir, they witnessed Carol's disappearance right before their very eyes. They could helps give us clues to catch whoever is responsible."

The finger quickly turned into a fist and slammed onto his desk.

"God damn it, Craig." the sheriff shouted. "These are kids! Not detectives."

Alan looked at his sheriff in the eyes.

"They may be kids," Alan shouted back but not as loud as Barkley, "but don't forget that one of them happened to be the son of your former partner!"

There was a small silence and Barkley slowly looked away. He remembered the time he was partner with Jake's father, Jeremy Miller. They used to hang out together at one of the bars in Carlton City having a drink when they were off duty. They used to be swapping jokes, laugh and even played a few pranks. They became friends instantly until Barkley noticed that Jeremy was more involved with his work than what was even more important. His family was waiting at their home, scared and almost defenceless from the corruption outside their front door. One thing that being on the force had taught Barkley was that it is your job to protect the city, but you start with your own family. They need to be protected most. They want to see you coming home without a single scratch. They want you to be there with them and be someone whom they can trust. You are your family's hero.

But Jeremy did not think that. He thought that protecting the city would make an even better environment for his family. But after his wife and son moved to the quiet town of Greensburg, he could not leave his precinct.

"Detective Jeremy was a good man." Barkley said softly. "He was a good partner, excellent cop and my best friend. The only thing I despised of him was his priorities."

"Do you feel the same with his son?" Alan asked.

Barkley shrugged, following with a sigh.

"I don't know. I just don't like the idea of Jake becoming like his father. I mean sure, he might turn out to be a good cop, one day. But I hope he doesn't screw up like his father did."

"Knowing Jake all of my life on the force," Alan said. "I've never doubted him, ever."

Barkley looked back at his subordinate.

"But still, if those kids ever did get in our way of the investigation, I may hold you responsible."

Barkley had been known to go directly by the book when it comes to being an officer of the law. And strict as he was, he would have Alan's badge if something gets screwed up. The young deputy had been with the police force for nearly five years and he wouldn't want to lose his badge at all. As a matter of fact, Barkley was one year close to retirement and was about to give his position to Alan as being the official Sheriff of the Greensburg Police Department. He did not want to lose that opportunity, so he accepted his orders from the Sheriff and walked away, heading out of the station to go see Dr. William Cummings.

The sun had finally gotten down but just enough to fill the town with its warm, orange glow of the sunset. Though there were some places in Greensburg that it felt like late evening, but that didn't stop Jake for what he was going to do, that night. He was planning on sneaking pass the police guarding the school and look around the stage to where Carol Graham had vanished. He would have Alice to help him out as well but she told him to wait until it was completely dark. He was determined to find out the truth of it all, about the disappearances and that shadowy thing that attacked him last night. And from what Old Man Peterson had told him about the time he saw something grabbing Karen Hannah before she was killed, it almost sounded similar to the event that happened in his bedroom.

Jake was sitting on the couch watching TV when Laura walked down the stairs with some cash in hand. She walked over to the kitchen and opened a cupboard above her head to reveal a giant jar full of money labelled 'Jake's College savings.' That jar had been around since Jake's mother moved into town and began to save some change to pay for Jake's education. The jar was about one-quarter full, and they planned to have it sent when the mountain of money would reach the top, nearly at the rim.

Laura place a five-dollar bill, closed the lid tight, and placed it back in the cupboard above her.

"We're almost there, Jake." His aunt said almost anxious. "A few more litres of cash and it would be enough to pay for your college."

Jake took a small g, nodded and turned his eyes back to the TV, watching a series of advertisements that almost made him laugh. He still had not decided on what course to take in college but his interest in writing stories, he was sure that there is a course where he can learn on how to be a professional author of detective novels. From his thoughts, he rather write about them then becoming one like his father and get shot to death by criminals.

Laura noticed that his nephew wasn't paying too much attention, and gave a certain look that he had so much thoughts in mind. Laura assumed it was from what happened in his bedroom, even though she did not see anything when she heard the ruckus.

"You okay, Jake?" she asked as she approached him behind his sofa.

"Yeah," the silent nephew replied. "I just want to know what's going on in this town."

Laura kissed the top of his head.

"I know, honey. So do I."

"I'm gonna go out for a bit, later. Hang out with Alice."

Laura smirked and gave him a nudge.

"You like her, don't you?"

Jake returned the smirk.

"Yeah, you can say that."

"Hey, I've seen you two looking at each other a few times. You two really connect."

"But the problem is that Jason's dating her. So basically, we're just friends. If I ever try to make a move on her, he's gonna become green and smash me into pulp. You know how he is."

A slight laugh had escaped Laura's breath.

"Oh well. Maybe by the time you attend college, you'll meet the right girl."

Laura walked back to the kitchen. Jake had thought about meeting others at college, but Alice had always been on his mind. From her glamorous figure to her kind, warm, gentleness of her soul, it would be difficult to find another girl like that. He would ask her to go on a date with her and for as long as they known each other throughout their school life, Alice would have definitely accept it. But there was a wall guarding her. A muscular, hulking wall that went by the name of Jason Baker. He made sure that Alice was his girlfriend and he doesn't care if he had to risk his own life for her. Even though he was a bit of hot head when it comes to sports and using that to add more toughness to his attitude, he would stick by Alice. She would be an excellent cheerleader at his first football game, if she had not chose to become a fashion designer. Those two were made for each other, Jake had thought. And he knew that he was destined to be alone.

Chapter 7

The house of Doctor William Cummings rested near the northern edge of Greensburg and close to the campgrounds. The house itself was the average white with black roofing but it also had a huge backyard lush with green grass and a small garden laying in the middle. It was a peaceful place for a chemistry teacher as well as a potential place for experimenting botany.

Dr. Cummings was standing near his garden showering the plants with cool water mixed with plant food. He was enjoying the warm evening that had fallen onto the town, while still emitting some light from sun. Though his moment of bliss was interrupted by the sound a car driving into the driveway. William looked and noticed it was a police patrol car, driven by deputy Alan Craig.

The young policeman climbed out and waved at the chemistry teacher Greensburg High School. The forty-year-old man waved back with a calm smile.

"Doctor Cummings." Alan called out. "Could I have a few minutes with you?"

"Sure," the teacher replied. "Go on in, make yourself at home. I'll be there in a bit."

The interior of the house had a lot of space for a single man to live in. Though it was a shame that both him and his wife used to live in that same house. Her picture was sat neatly on a shelf just above living room fireplace along with other photos of him and his wife together. When Alan looked at those photos, he did felt sad that his wife had dicd a long timc ago and he was having a hard time coping with that terrible loss. And to have Karen Hannah doing a psychiatric evaluation would seem right for the teacher, if there were nothing else involved during that session.

Dr. Cummings walked into the house through the patio doors and found Alan looking at the photos near the fireplace.

"My wife and I," he pointed out.

Alan nodded, still looking at the beautiful, young-looking smile through the photo.

"She is beautiful. And I'm sorry about what happened to her."

"I had such hard time dealing with her death that I was literally falling apart. I almost even thought of killing myself just so I can see her again. But I would thank Karen Hannah for helping me dealing with my problems."

William's eyes lowered, thinking that since Karen is dead, he won't be thanking her again.

"That's why I'm here, Doctor . It's about you and Karen."

William's eyes went back to Alan, but with somewhat raised heart beat and was very slowly began to have heavy breathing.

"Oh?" the chemistry teacher said. "You wouldn't think I'd killed that poor child?"

Alan shook his head.

"No. The way she died would be impossible for any of us to accomplish. I'm talking about that session you two have had."

William sat at the nearby chair in the living room without saying a word. With that Alan noticed that his silence had meant that he actually did something but he needed to clarify and confirmed that what he read on that speech that Karen had written was true.

"You were there when Carol Graham vanished during the power outage, during the graduation ceremony. Am I correct?"

"Yes."

"Did you know that the rest of the speech that Karen had prepared was supposed to be her confession?"

He didn't say anything except slowly shook his head. He wouldn't know anything about the confession that Karen would give to the townspeople. But thinking about having her secrets exposed had made him a bit more nervous and a bit more worried.

82

"Well, in that confession she wrote, in that speech, it said that she did a psychiatric evaluation on you. And according to how it was written, there was more to it than that."

William was getting more nervous and his hands slowly began to tighten his knees. Alan stared into the chemistry teacher's eyes and asked him a question that made 's heart unsettling.

"Doctor," he said. "Did you had sex with Karen Hannah during the psychiatric session?"

He let out a nervous laugh.

"What are you talking about?"

"You know Karen was only sixteen when she was killed. If you did had sex with her, you know very well that it's a crime."

William had no words to evade Alan's interrogation. He decided to give up on the effort and told Alan what happened.

"She seduced me." he spoke softly.

Alan was puzzled to what he said.

"Seduced you?"

"She was using my own pain to her advantage. She told me that if I give the recommendation for the scholarship, she wouldn't tell a single soul about our...session."

"What do you mean she seduced you?"

"It was a really a psychiatric session to begin with. I had such a difficult time dealing with the loss of my wife that she had offered me her assistance. I knew that she wanted to be a fully licensed psychiatrist so I accepted her offer."

William's hands had finally stopped gripping on his knees. It did felt painful at first but remembering that time with Karen was even more dreadful to him, since she was using his own pain of losing his wife to her own advantage and seduced him.

"I was telling her how I felt about losing my wife," began. "Hearing the phone call when I was enjoying some wine and classical music, saying that she was in an accident and did everything they can to save her. She died the next day."

He let out a big sigh.

"What else?"

The chemistry teacher's eyes suddenly began to be filled with tears.

"When I told her everything, she walked up to me while I was laying down on the sofa. She told me that killing myself would bring more pain and suffering and my wife wouldn't even want that from me. So, she convinced me that if I keep her alive in my memories and in my heart, she is never gone."

The tears had finally began to trickle down his cheeks.

"Did she do anything during that time?" Alan asked

 William nodded.

"She wanted to make me feel better, making me not sad anymore. I didn't know what she was talking about until..."

"Until what?"

"Until she kissed me."

Alan had thought it over. Did she wanted to go that far to becoming a fully licensed psychiatrist? This had made his brain twist in different directions. Who would have thought that a sweet, kind, determined child like Karen Hannah would do something like that?.

"After she kissed me," continued, "she said she would help me if I do the same for her. She said if we kept that part of the session between us, I would given the recommendation for a scholarship in psychiatry. I didn't understand what she meant she began to....touch me."

William remembered Karen touching him sensually and even remembering it all had made him uncomfortable.

"She began to say certain words, certain phrases. I couldn't even make out what she was saying. I was mesmerized by her seductive ways, her sweet talk and kept on touching me, caressing me. And while she was doing all that, it reminded me of the times I had with my wife. Karen was smiling, spoke to me softly, just like her. I would have thought the heavens had given me the chance to be with her."

Alan stood there trying to get all that information in. Picturing Karen doing something like that to her chemistry teacher was hard enough to believe. But the fact that she was only sixteen when she seduced him, and using her ways to get inside his head and believed it was his dead wife in front of his eyes. So it almost became clear that Dr. Cummings was not to blame for that sort of misconduct.

"When I came to, she was already gone and left a note near me. It said that if I don't give her some sort of scholarship for her future studies, then she would tell the entire faculty about the 'extra time' we had."

Alan stood there, quiet as ever. A slight nod was barely visible from the young deputy.

"I didn't know what to do or what was going through my mind. I had no choice but to give the recommendation to the principal of the school for the scholarship. I would lose my job, and even end up in prison for 'frolicking' with a minor."

Alan had heard enough from what the chemistry teacher had told him. It was crystal clear that it wasn't his fault that he had sex with a minor. Karen had done it all. She used her skills as a psychiatrist to get inside his head and used it to her advantage just to get ahead in her studies. It almost made Alan sick in his stomach about how some people would go that far to achieve their dreams instead of working toward them. Karen was a lying, cheating, and selfish student. As for Carol Graham who helped her, she may have been as well.

"Don't worry about a thing, Dr. Cummings." Alan said. "I'll make sure they won't lock you up."

Alan began to walk toward the front door of the house but stopped half-way.

"You really do miss your wife."

William nodded.

"Well, I'm gonna head back. If there's anything else you need to tell me, just give a call at the station."

Alan was almost at the door when William spoke again.

"You know, it's funny." he said. "Karen wasn't the only person who was carrying a smile similar to my wife's."

Alan turned his head back, curious about what he just said.

"Really?"

The teacher nodded.

"About a week after my wife died, two days after I came to this town and began my job as a teacher, I sometimes go for a walk around the school grounds watching children playing. All the boys and girls were having a fun time. And the smiles on their faces were priceless. But the smiles on those little girls were more than that. Each of them reminded me of my wife. Elegant, beautiful and full of life, it was like I can see her in every face."

He began to sob silently.

Alan looked at the crying teacher. He did not realized how long had suffered since the death of wife, but from the way he had said about little girls wearing her smile almost made him question the teacher's thoughts. He was thinking about asking him but seeing him sobbing had prevented him from questioning even further except taking a look at the garden and the small shack in the backyard.

"What's that your growing?" he asked.

William wiped the tears off and swallowed some of sobbing.

"Oh, um..." stuttered, "I'm just growing some potatoes. My father used to be a farmer for the Greensburg Agricultural Company when I was little. He taught me how to grow potatoes and everything there is to know about gardening."

"What about that shack?"

Alan had noticed the shack behind the garden had a huge wooden sign with the words 'Keep Out' written in white pain.

"Oh that's where I keep my botany experiments. I'm conducting some sort of research about isolation and outside oxygen."

"Is that why you have a 'Keep Out' sign on the front door?"

"I only put it there because it's sealed from any outdoor environment. The oxygen would ruin whatever I'm currently working on in there but it's only temporary."

Alan made a slight nod as he got up from the chair walked toward the kitchen.

"Well," Alan said as he opened the door. "Sorry to have bother you. If there is anything you give us a call."

Alan was already out of the door into the night when he suddenly forgot to say something else to the chemistry teacher so he went back in.

"Oh, and I would advise you to..." Alan was stopped in his tracks when he suddenly saw something wrapping around William's body.

"Holy shit!" Alan exclaimed.

A dark, shadowy figure that was on a wall behind the teacher, twice his size, had wrapped around his neck and torso like a squid. His mouth was opened but was stuffed with another shadowy tentacle, probing down his throat as he gagged relentlessly. He was getting pulled toward the figure as the surface of it looked like waves of black, crude liquid.

Alan ran up to the helpless chemistry teacher and pulled onto his outreached arm. The force of the shadowy entity was very strong, stronger than him, even more than Sheriff Barkley. He tried to get to break free by prying the black tentacles off of him but they were too attached to his body.

Alan kept on pulling when he suddenly heard faint giggling noises coming from the black figure, as if several children were laughing and enjoying the whole ordeal. Finally, those giggling sounds grew louder and several children appeared. Emerged from the black, wavy pool were faces of little girls. Their eyes were bright yellow and their entire skin covered in the same black liquid. Alan was able to count them out, which it was ten little girls that appeared before him. But they looked familiar. Each of the ten faces looked similar to the missing children posters pinned up near his desk at the police station.

Alan began to lose his grip as the ten little girls reached out with their little dark hands and gotten a hold of every inch on William. The extra hands were more than enough to pull the teacher into the black pool and with Alan suddenly lost his grip, the chemistry teacher from Greensburg High School had finally sunk into the black, oily pool that was swarming on the wall. As soon as had gone through, it hardened itself and the shape of the figure remain printed on the wall.

As Alan saw the giant, black print left behind, it was similar to the ones found at Karen Hannah's bedroom and the stage floor. And those children he saw, similar to the ones that went missing. Alan asked himself why did they appear and grabbed Dr. William Cummings and what was his connection to them. But he could not find an answer since he cannot think straight.

The radio barked from his right side. Alan grabbed the microphone from his left shoulder strap and spoke into it, stuttering with fear and confusion.

"Craig, here." he said.

"Alan," the radio barked. "You better come over to the station. We found the missing boy, and I believe the parents wont be happy to hear the bad news."

Chapter 8

Greensburg town was finally pitch black. Several homes were seen with no light shining through their windows and the people inside them were sleeping soundly in their beds. The children were dreaming of several imaginative things, like what they want to be when they become older. Jake wanted to be like his father, a police detective. But after he was shot and killed, his mind kind of shifted. He was not sure if that was what he really wanted. Risking your life to protect a crime-filled city and the denizens that walked along the filthy streets. But one thing that stayed with him was his will to keep going and felt some dedication to find out the truth. He had to, his classmates vanished with only one of them found dead in an unnatural way and he would go so far as to cross the yellow tape that surrounded the perimeter of the school. Not only that, he had to bring Alice with him as well.

Jake and Alice walked up the street toward the school. Not only there were yellow 'no crossing' tape around the school, but there were a few guarding police officers roaming around the area. When the school was finally in view, they stopped.

"We need to get passed the patrol if we're gonna check out the gym's stage." Jake said quietly to Alice.

"Are you crazy?" she said with an almost loud voice. "How are we gonna do that?"

Jake shook his head. It would be impossible and imprudent to go into the building through the main entrance with two officers guarding it. As well as the double doors not far from it which led directly into the gym. The grey metal doors on both left and right side of the school also had a guarding officer. But like almost every plan of entry, the back door would suffice.

Jake and Alice turned right on another street but kept their distance from the patrolling guards to make them believe they were not gonna walk toward the yellow tape. As soon as they were a bit further away, Jake grabbed Alice's goat and directed her through an open field. They hid behind a picket fence and peered outward, trying to get a g of anyone guarding the back entrance. Unfortunately there was a policeman guarding the back door.

"That's mostly where the janitors enter the school," Jake pointed out in a whisper.

"Now, what?" Alice whispered, feeling disappointed about the whole thing.

Jake slightly shook his head. Suddenly, his wandering eyes had spotted a grey-coloured cat walking by on the other side of the fence. The cat had belonged to an old lady who lived near the field. She called the cat 'Wiggles' because its tail was always wiggling when it is happy. It had red collar with the cat's name printed on it as well as a little bell.

The cat spotted Jake and Alice and meowed softly. It's tail began wiggling, feeling happy to see two humans playing hide and seek behind the white fence. But when the cat and Jake stared into each other's eyes, Jake bit his lip. He had an idea on how to get by the guard. It may be bad for Wiggles, but it was some idea that Jason Baker had came up with when he wanted to steal some bottles of vodka from the liquor store. Luckily the cat was very light in terms of weight and the length was sufficient for carrying one-handed. He then looked around the area and noticed some garbage cans in a corner of the street, from where they had walked from.

"I got an idea," Jake whispered.

"What?" Alice replied as Jake picked up the cat from the other side of the fence. "What are you going to do with that poor thing?"

"Something crazy. As soon as the guard walks away from the door, we go up there as fast but quietly as possible."

The officer guarding the back door of the school yawned heavily. He had been on duty for several hours and could not wait until his replacement to arrive. Surrounded by a faint light from a small lamp attached to the brick wall, it was illuminating the doors but the guarding officer's face was barely seen by the darkness of night covering his features. He was nearly about to doze off while leaning against the metal doors when he was suddenly jumped by a screeching cry of a cat and a tumbling sound of large tin cans near by. The cry was loud and ear shattering as if the poor four-legged animal had just lost its tail. The tumbling noise sounded like a pair of trash cans from a nearby corner of the street.

"What the fuck gave you that idea to throw that poor cat into the trashcan?" Alice whispered angrily.

"Blame it on your boyfriend." Jake replied while reaching in his jacket pocket. "He was the one who came up with the idea in the first place."

Jake remembered it well. When he and Jason was in eight grade, Jason had dared Jake to help him with his booze-snatching plan. They would sneak up to the liquor store with a cat at the ready and Jason would throw it into a nearby trash receptacle. The crashing sound and the cat's screeching cry would startle the store clerk and would check to see where the sound had came from. When the store clerk walked out of the store and toward the toppled trashcans, Jake and Jason would quickly slip in and grab what they can before the clerk traverse back through the door.

Jake had pulled out a leather folding pouch from his jacket pocket. When he opened the pouch, metal, skinny rods with hooks and screws at their ends were revealed underneath. It was his father's lock pick set. He used them on some of his cases before, and had given the set to his son just before he and his mother moved out from the city. He told his son that sometimes you need to have lock picks. Because sometimes potential suspects would hide certain things in their homes like safes or cabinets. And there are times where you have to break into their homes to find the truth, despite not having a search warrant. As for Jake, he wanted to find the truth himself. He thought that it is possible the Greensburg Police Department may have overlooked something in the gymnasium. But after what he had experienced in his bedroom and what Old Man Peterson told him, he was certain that they did.

He took two lock picks and inserted them into the lock of the door.

"All you got to do is keep on pressing on that little lever." Jake told Alice.

The doors had no knob, just a hand grip and a thumb lever above it, similar to the ones you might find at a store or any public building. Alice kept pressing on the thumb lever while Jake continued jiggling around the guts of the lock.

"Hurry up, Jake." Alice whispered loudly. "He'll be back in any minute."

"Almost got it." Jake said.

The picks had suddenly locked into place and both made a ninety-degree turn to the right. The thumb lever had became lighter and Alice was able to push it down, and listen to the sound of the latch sliding away from the inside. The metal door had finally swung open allowing Jake and Alice to quickly slip inside and quietly close it to avoid any other distractions by the nearby guards.

They were finally inside but the hallways were dark with very limited light from the emergency lights above them. Jake and Alice looked around to find a way to get to the gymnasium through the darkness.

"How are we gonna find the gym if we can't see where we are?" Alice whispered.

"The gym shouldn't be too far." Jake explained. "Since we came from the back door, should be a hallway on our right that leads down to the white corridor."

Jake pulled out a flashlight that was the size of a ball point pen. It gave a blueish glow and had enough lighting power to reveal a small portion of the tiled floor. He turned to his right and began walking as he scanned around his area with his flashlight. Alice followed but very closely and cautiously, hoping that nothing would jump out of the darkness and make her turn white. Jake surveyed some more until he suddenly spotted something faintly white down the hallway. He pointed his flashlight on it and it revealed a white, concrete wall.

"There it is." Jake said

The corridor was all painted white with only two doors on each side. The doors on the far end were one of the entrances to the gym while the other is the girls, change room. As for the doors that were closest to Jake and Alice, the one on the left was a 'Home Economics' classroom and the right was another entrance to the gym. Since that door was located on the right side of the gym's stage, Jake would go for that one. As he and Alice quickly walked up to the door, he checked to see in the door was locked. Conveniently, it wasn't. It swung open easily and the two had finally got in.

There were no lights in the gymnasium. Only the emergency lights attached to the exit signs above the other doors were lit but not well enough to expose the stage.

"We're just gonna need the stage lights." Jake said to Alice as he climbed up on the stage, still pointing his flashlight at certain spots.

The panel for the lights were well hidden in a wall between the parted curtains and the drapes behind the stage. Jake pointed the light at the panel and swung the steel door open. There were several switches but Jake remembered which one was the stage lights, since he used to be part of the school's drama club. He found the switch and flipped it.

The four bright lights beamed down on the stage evaporating the darkness and exposed the stage floor and the podium that was left there since the graduation ceremony. Not only that, the black print from where Carol Graham had left when she vanished during the power outage was still plainly visible on the varnished stage floor. Luckily, the police did not break the stage floor to check if Carol would be underneath like Karen was, but they said that they went in the storage compartments which was accessed through the compartment doors on the front of the stage. It was used for storing chairs and portable balconies, similar to the ones Jake and Alice had sat on during their graduation.

Carol's black print still remained, visibly shaped as if she would still be standing at the podium giving out Karen Hannah's speech to the crowd in front of her. Thinking about what happened that day still haunted Jake's thoughts and memories along with that giant, black entity that attacked him.

Alice climbed up the stage and looked at the print.

"My, God." Alice said. "What do you think happened?"

Jake shook his head while looking around the stage. He was searching around for anything that may prove him wrong that there was some sort of supernatural occurrence that happened during that day. Alice knelt down near the print and slightly touched it with her fingers. The print was cold, even colder than ice. She then touched the floor itself about an inch away from the print and the wooden surface was very warm.

"Any idea who or what could have done this?" Alice asked Jake.

"I don't know." Jake replied still looking around. "I'm pretty sure what happened here occurred the same way with Karen. I just want to know how."

Jake suddenly gave up and let out a big sigh. He couldn't find anything that would give him a clue about the disappearances and felt that sneaking into the gymnasium, avoiding the police, and even searching for the truth behind these events would be for nothing.

He looked back at the black print and up toward the stage lights, just about to throw the towel until something in his brain had triggered a memory. The memory of when he was attacked in his bedroom by that black figure. He felt a cool breeze before that thing grabbed him and he remembered looking behind him to where he saw his shadow on the door of his bedroom. He also remembered when he looked again and his shadow had grew. Could it be just a coincidence? Jake was willing to find that out.

Jake quickly inspected Carol Graham's print. It was stretched out from the base of the podium to nearly six feet in length. It was strange because Carol had worn small white shoes with golden butterflies. She had never wore any high-heels.

"Alice," Jake called her. "How tall do you think Carol is?"

Alice was a bit puzzled by the question. "About my height, five-feet six why?"

"If Carol is about five-feet six, then why is the print the same height as a basketball player?"

Jake then suddenly looked up at the stage lights and back down.

"Could you stand in front of the podium, like as if you were giving the speech?"

Alice did what he asked. She stood in front of the podium. Jake's eyes widened when he glanced both the stage lights and then Carol's print, that was then overlapped by Alice's shadow. Both her shadow and the print matched almost exactly and because of the angle that the stage lights were at, her shadow would stretch out making it as long as Carol's print itself.

"That's what I thought." Jake said with a confirming nod. "Carol had been taken away from us by her own shadow."

Alice looked at him, hoping what he said was just crazy talk.

"If she's taking away by her own shadow," she said, "how come Karen's body was found but not Carol's?"

Jake was just about to answer her but they were startled by a slamming sound of the front doors of the gymnasium. One of the patrolling policeman had burst right through the metal doors with a flashlight shining on their faces.

"What the hell you kids doing here?" the policeman shouted. "This is a crime scene!"

Both Alice and Jake slowly raised their hands. The two were finally caught and Alice nearly felt like hitting Jake in the back of his head for having her tagged along. She would imagine her dream being a fashion designer getting thrown out of the window all because of one of her friend's crazy search for a killer shadow. Instead she just nudged him in his back.

"You owe me on, Jake." Alice said to her accomplice. "You owe me one, big time!"

Back at the Greensburg Police station, Sheriff Barkley was burning red, and barking like a rabid dog who had his bone stolen.

"So let me get this straight," the sheriff shouted. "You mean to tell me that Dr. William Cummings, the chemistry teacher had been kidnapped by a ghost?"

"It wasn't a ghost, sir." Alan said, almost at the same voice level as his superior. "But I know what I saw."

"Did it came out of his shadow like some sort of black thing?" Jake asked his best friend.

"Yeah. Not only that, there were ten little girls that came out of that thing. They do look like the same ten girls that went missing."

"This is complete bullshit!" Barkley snapped, throwing his hat onto the desk. "We got a dead three-year-old who's most likely got ran over by a vehicle, I got two kids that interfered with official police business and pretty much compromised a crime scene, and I have a deputy who he thinks he saw the big black bogeyman!"

"But sir..."

"That's enough out of you, deputy Craig! Lock up those two in the hallway!"

"No!" Alan snapped back.

Barkley nearly re-act to Alan's refusal of the direct order he gave him.

"Alice is my sister and my responsibility. She was just dragged into it. I'll just take her home."

"If she is your responsibility, then that makes you responsible for letting it all happen. And to think I was gonna give up my position as the law of this town to you.   Now I realized I was gonna give it up to someone one who's head is not screwed on straight."

Alan did not uttered a single word to the sheriff of Greensburg. He knew that Clarence Barkley would not listen to what Alan had said about Dr. Cummings and the black entity that snatched him away. No one would believe him anyways, except Jake, since he had an experience like that before.

"Your suspended until further notice." Barkley said with a slightly calmer but disappointed voice. "Give me your gun and your badge."

Alan just stood there in silence with his eyes fixed on the sheriff, nearly felt like ripping his old throat off.

"Now!" Barkley shouted.

The young deputy had finally done what his sheriff ordered. He unhooked the gun holster from his belt and laid it down on his desk. As for his badge, he unbutton it from his uniform and threw it at Barkley. The sheriff caught it, but his face slightly flinched by the feeling of the sharp-pointed pin that had pierced his palm.

"Let's go, Alice." Alan said softly to his sister as they both walked out of the station.

Jake just stood there as he watched his two friends disappear through the doors. Alice only looked back once but for just a brief second. Jake knew he was gonna be in trouble for disobeying the police about interfering with their business but just like his father, we was still determined to find out what was going on on the town.

Sheriff Barkley walked up to Jake with piercing eyes.

"I don't know what your trying to pull, son." Barkley said, nearly growling. "But you are not your dad. Your not even a cop. You may have his determination but don't let that go over your head. He was good cop and a find friend, but he was too self-confident in his job that he completely forgot about what was really important to him. And like I said, it takes special training to become a detective. But until you do that, you will follow my orders as a civilian and do not get in my way. Is that clear, Jake?"

Jake nodded, giving the sheriff a cold stare.

"Now, since you disobeyed me for going into a crime scene, I'm afraid I'm gonna have to lock you up. Don't worry, you won't be sharing a cell with Old Man Peterson after that fiasco this morning."

Sheriff Barkley directed Jake into the hallway. Dark, damp and the smell of wet concrete had rammed into his nose like a pair of bullet trains. He was used to that smell, since he got busted one time for stealing the bottles of booze from the liquor store with Jason Baker. The cells were large enough to put almost five people in, but just like the town sheriff had said, he wasn't going to put Jake in the same jail cell as Old Man Peterson. The wet concrete wall was good enough to separate them.

Barkley had slid the jail door shut and locked it with a large key.

"I would suggest get some sleep." Barkley. "I'm gonna give your aunt a call and have her pick you up in the morning."

Jake laid down on the bed. It wasn't as filthy as the one in Peterson's cell, but was uncomfortable and Jake had no choice but to take his coat off and fold it into a pillow to lay his head on. While he was laying there, several thoughts had passed through his mind. One was about his father, then his mother's suicide, Karen Hannah's death, Carol's disappearance, and the thought that the prints both Karen and Carol had left behind were actually their own shadows.

How could that be possible, he thought. But when he went through his experience with the black figure in his mind, it was slowly became clear that their shadows had somehow came alive and grabbed them. Only difference is that Jake saw his mother in his own shadow and Alan said he saw the ten missing girls in Dr. Cumming's shadow. And for what Old Man Peterson had described about girly hands coming out of Karen Hannah's assailant, it would be possible that the assailant was indeed her own shadow. As for Carol Graham, it was difficult to tell since she was snatched away when the electricity of the entire school had gone out. But with Alice's help and having nearly the same height as Carol, it was very clear that Karen's best friend had been kidnapped by her own shadow as well.

But then, there was Karen's remains. A skeleton covered in black bile. That was what made Jake lose track in his thoughts in all of the events that occurred. All of these disappearance and only one body was found. He couldn't do anything at the moment. All he could do was to sit tight in his cell, hoping that the morning would make him feel a bit better than he was.

But what Alan would tell to his sister about the three-year-old that the sheriff had mentioned, Alice's hope of relief from it all had been postponed.

Chapter 9

Sheriff Barkley drove to an estate which belonged to the chemistry teacher, Dr. William Cummings. According to what his former deputy had told him, had been snatched away and disappeared right in front of his eyes. To Barkley, that would be crazy talk, but when he walked into the house and noticed the black print on the wall in the kitchen, he was nearly a believer. He never believed in all of the supernatural crap. When something like that occurred, he always looked for any rational explanation. Like someone had use black smoke, carved a man-sized hole in the wall and grabbed Cummings. But when Alan had mentioned about the ten little girls who he claimed to be the same girls who were reported missing, he shook his head saying that he may have been overworked.

The yellow tape had stretched across 's estate and several officers were wondering around searching for any leads that may indicate the doctor's whereabouts. Barkley looked around the kitchen some more and turned his head toward the dinning room. At the back of the dining room was a patio door and a small garden with a wooden shed was revealed through the double paned glass from the backyard of the house.

One of the officers walked up to the sheriff.

"Just like the other two, sir." the deputy said. "Vanished without a trace except for that black stain on the wall."

"Did you check that shack?" Barkley asked.

"Larry's getting a crowbar to open it up. It's sealed really tight."

Outside in the backyard, deputy Larry Fisher and another officer walked up to the tool shed with a crowbar handy. Larry began to pry off the hinges, but even the hinges were off, the door was still shut tight. So he tired to slid the flatten end of the crowbar between the door and the doorway and pulled on with help from his partner.

The door had finally popped opened. The interior side of the door was covered in plastic wrapping and duct tape. But with the tool shed now opened, a foul stench had rammed into the two officer's nose. The smell was horrendous, like a mixture of urine, and feces and rotten garbage. There was no way that Cummings would have done some experimental botany with a stench like that.

Deputy Larry took out his flashlight and shined the light into the interiors of the wooden shack. As he and his partner walked in, they noticed that there was no sign of plant life, not even a single vine. The entire interior of the shack was completely covered in plastic wrapping, bubble wrapping, duct tape, clear tape and an old rusted bed with a filthy mattress on it and a pair of shackles and some old rope laying on top. The two officers assumed that the horrible smell may have come from the mattress, as it was discoloured with dried urine and even showed some traces of dried blood.

Near the bed was a tripod holding a small video camera pointing toward the bed. And not far from that was a metal shelf with several cases of cassette tapes each with a title on their bindings. The whole shack looked like a dungeon, and the video cassettes and camera indicated that Dr. Cummings had something hidden away, something sinister and possibly a very terrible sin he had kept away for several years.

Larry kept scanning around with the light when his partner nudged him.

"Look." he said. "On those tapes. There's names on them."

Larry shined his light on the series of video tapes and they all revealed several names: 'Sharon Lake and the Doctor,' 'Lindsey Cameron and the Doctor,' 'Amanda Connelly and the Doctor.' Those names had rang a bell for Larry. Those first three names were three of the ten missing little girls. He kept going through all the names until one had made him stop, and stood there froze in shock.

'Alexandra Fisher and the Doctor,' was what the deputy saw on one of those tapes. Alexandra was Larry's ten-year-old daughter. She went missing about month before the whole incident of Karen Hannah's death. But seeing her name on the title had given him a shiver up his back and a random outcome into his mind.

Larry grabbed the video tape with his latex glove on and walked toward the video camera. He didn't assume that the camera still had some battery power left, but it was very close of dying out. He opened the cassette box, placed the tape into the camera and pressed the play button.

A video display was attached to the camera showing some footage of what was on. What Larry had seen through the display had made his hands turned into fists, his eyes filled with tears and his head filled with anger. Thoughts of finding Dr. Cummings and put a bullet into his head were the first thing that went through his head. For what the chemistry had done to his daughter, he would kill him. No matter if he was an officer of the law or a normal citizen of Greensburg, Larry Fisher would kill Dr. Cummings with his own hands.

The display showed a little, curly, brunette in a blue flowered dress sucking on a lollipop. Her faint expression she had gave away assumed that she may have been drugged by whatever what in the lollipop. She sat there on the bed when a figure of a man walked into view. It was Dr. Cummings, staring eagerly into the child. There was no sound coming from the camera so it is impossible to hear what the chemistry teacher was saying to the poor girl.

The doctor then sat next to the girl and slightly pulled her innocent face toward his. Since the girl was under the effects of the drug from the candy, her eyes were not fixed on his, just wandering off as if she was under some sort of trance. spoke once more but again, there was no sound coming from the video. A moment later, the lips of Larry Fisher's missing ten-year-old daughter was about an inch away from but the last ounce of battery life had taken its toll and the video was cut off.

Deputy Larry Fisher had tears running down his face. It was a good thing that he did not see the rest of the footage, since the last of it was pretty much what he assumed the chemistry teacher had done to his daughter. He would not bare to watch the rest as it would be disturbing enough. He palm was over his eyes trying to block some of the tears as his partner patted on his back for comfort. Poor Alexandra. Where could she had gone?

Meanwhile, outside in the backyard, Sheriff Barkley was staring at the that Cummings was growing. The plant leaves were enormous and the flowers were bloomed with such life that he remembered giving a bouquet of flowers to his wife before he proposed to her for marriage.

It made him smile for a bit, but it quickly disappeared for when his eyes had spotted something sticking out of the dark soil.

He crouched down and parted away some of the leaves. The white, ivory object that was sticking out of the soil was plainly seen and with slightly touching it, it felt hard and smooth at the same time. It was a piece of a bone. But Dr. Cummings had no dog since he was allergic to certain pets.

"Someone get me a shovel!" Barkley ordered.

One of the deputies gave a shovel to his superior and Barkley began to dig into the garden. About half an hour later, the entire garden   was transformed into a hidden stash of several skeletons, possibly ten of them. All of them are which they appeared small and their skulls had a huge, cracked hole in them.

Deputy Larry Fisher walked out of the shack, still recovering from his tears and saw the little skeletons in the garden. Most of them still had torn and filthy clothes on but Larry recognized some of the clothing. One of them was a torn, blue dress with flowers decorated on them, the same dress that his ten-year-old daughter wore on the recording that Dr. Cummings had made. With the horror of seeing his daughter on video and her remains hidden neatly underneath the garden, Larry fell to his knees and more tears had flushed out of his hazel eyes.

Dr. Cummings, chemistry teacher of Greensburg High School had kidnapped ten little girls between ages eight and ten, held them in the little shack for his personal and illicit purpose and killed them to prevent the children from saying anything to the public. And now that the chemistry teacher had vanished leaving nothing but a large black print of himself on the wall, sheriff Clarence Barkley and deputy Larry Fisher thought that whatever had happened to the troubled teacher, he absolutely deserved it.

Chapter 10

The streets were even darker than ever. Houses, mailboxes and dog houses were less visible in the distance as the curtain of night shrouded them away and kept them silent and tranquil in the dark. Only the warm glowing light from the street lamps had kept most of the darkness at bay. Moths fluttering around them as the citizens of Greensburg were tucked in their beds, dreaming of a future and hoping that each day, their dreams would be fulfilled. The streets were quiet but only Alice and Alan were left, walking down the street heading home.

"I'm sorry, Alan." Alice said to her brother, feeling responsible for for getting him suspended form the Greensburg Police Department.

"It's not your fault, sis." Alan replied with a comforting smile. "To be honest, I'm glad I'm out of Barkley's hands. He may be a good sheriff of the town, but he's not the type you would have a few drinks at the bar with."

Sheriff Clarence Barkley had every reason to be strict and to his job directly by the book. If it weren't for that incident when he was back at the precinct in Carlton City, he would have been an excellent role model to the town and bit more supportive. He and his partner Jeremy Miller were about to get something to eat when the convenience store from across the street was suddenly shaken by several gunshots from the inside.

Two armed robbers with black ski masks emerged from the store carrying a bag of money and food. One robber was tall and built was carrying a 9mm pistol while the other, shorter and scrawny was carrying a micro-Uzi. Without any hesitation, Jeremy got to the car and called on the radio for back-up while Clarence went after the two armed robbers.

They were already half-a-mile away from Clarence's reach so he decided to cut them off through the nearby alleyways. As soon as they met, the robbers turned tail in the opposite direction and began shooting. Clarence took cover behind a large dumpster, avoiding the incoming bullets. Sparks fly when they hit the metal surface of the dumpster and particles of brick and plaster nearly flew into his face.

The scrawny gunman kept firing his micro-Uzi at the cowering detective. But when the opportunity came, Clarence took his standard-issued 9mm automatic and squared his sights on him. He just wanted to do a take-down shot, so he was aiming for one of his shoulders. After getting shot at several times, he was shaken and having a difficult time keeping the gun steady. The scrawny gunman shot back, making Clarence losing his concentration and fire his handgun.

The assailant went down fast as his partner looked back for a brief second and continued running, leaving him to the cop. As Clarence walked over, he noticed that he shot the scrawny gunman in the back of his skull. The hollow point bullet had been broken up when it made impact with the skull and shredded the brain, exited as a puff of red and pink cloud, shutting down his nervous system and killing him instantly. When he rolled the body over and took off the black ski mask, he froze in shock to who it was underneath.

A young, fourteen-year-old face was revealed and Clarence had recognized him from the children's hospital. He had suffered from major burns in his body due to a fire accident at his house. The fire was electrical and the flames had overwhelmed him, refusing him to escape. Clarence was the one who had saved him from the fire, carrying his burning body to safety. He had saved his life from the fire, but he could not save him from a flying bullet.

"That's the reason why he came to this town." Alan explained. "He thought he would be calm and be living under a quiet and peaceful town, away from all the ruckus in the city. But I think the past is still haunting him, even as we speak."

"That's sad." Alice said. "Is he making up for it?"

Alan shook his head.

"I don't know. All I know is that every time I look at him, you can see an sign of guilt in his eyes. And I bet he wished he wasn't a policeman."

Alice then remembered something that the sheriff had said back in the station.

"What about that three-year-old they found in the woods?" she asked.

Alan let out a big sigh. "It turns out it was the little boy who was missing, the day after Karen's funeral. He was found hidden underneath some branches and leaves, deep in the forest. His head was crushed and there were tire marks on his clothes. It was clear that he got hit by an incoming vehicle."

"A hit and run?" Alice said. "That's terrible. But were there any witnesses?"

"Nobody witnessed the hit, but a young couple at a nearby camp heard a crash. They said they saw a blue pick-up truck that appeared to hit a tree. Then they claimed that the truck had backed up and the driver came out of the truck with a crowbar and did some extra damage to it. Smashed a headlight, ripped the front bumper off, and cracked the windshield."

"When did they saw that?"

"Yesterday, in the afternoon."

Alice had suddenly stopped walking and paused. She made a concerned look and remembered something that same day.

"Jason called me around that time saying he hit a moose on the way home from the city."

"Yeah..." Alan said, having the same concerned look. "And his dad's pick-up truck happens to be blue."

Alice was afraid to ask about the driver's description but she had to be sure.

"Did the couple told you what he looked like?" she asked her brother.

"They said he looked built, short blond hair." Alan replied. " Nearly the same size as a football player."

Alice thoughts were going haywire. That couldn't be possible, she thought. Jason may be stubborn and sometimes he may have a one-tracked mind, but for the length of time he and Alice had been together, he wouldn't do something something like that.

"I'm gonna go see Jason," Alice said bluntly. "I'll see you back home."

Alice turned toward a direction and began to walk quickly down the same road as Jason's house was located.

"Alice, wait a minute!" Alan cried out but her sister had ignored him.

She wanted answers and she was hoping that the thought having Jason run over a little boy and hid it from the authorities and covering his tracks was all a big mistake. But in order to keep her from any sort of harm, Alan decided to follow her at a certain distance.

Alice arrived at her boyfriend's home and noticed the garage door was opened. The pick-up truck that was stored inside was indeed painted blue, just like what Alan had told her. She walked around to the front and the front bumper was still missing, and the right headlight was shattered and the windshield was cracked. She walked back and noticed the steering column underneath the steering wheel was slightly crooked.

Jason had told her that he hit the moose hard enough that the engine had kicked out, unable to re-start the vehicle. Luckily, the side window on the driver's side was opened all the way and the locking latch was extended upwards, indicating that the door was unlocked. As she opened the door and took a closer look at the disturbed column underneath the steering wheel with a recollection of asking if Jason tried to hot-wire it. Her boyfriend said he hadn't tried, which made her feel more concerned than ever.

Alice reached out and took a good grip of the steering column. It suddenly came loose and was suddenly dropped to the black floor mat at the feet of the driver's seat. When she looked at what was underneath, her mouth nearly dropped all the way. A pair of yellow ignition wires were discovered but they were both cut.

"Alice?" a voice had startled her.

She quickly got out of the truck and noticed her boyfriend was standing at the front of the vehicle.

"Jason," she said to him.

"Is there something wrong?"

Jason stared into her girlfriend's concerned eyes. She looked afraid and somewhat shaken. But that was because she was scared of knowing the truth and hoping that all that she heard was not true.

"Jason," Alice said softly, but a little shaky. "Did you really hit a moose?"

"Yeah," replied. "Why? What's wrong?"

"Then how come your ignition wires are cut?"

Jason tried to say something but nothing came out.

"The police found a three-year-old boy dead in the woods. They said that his head was crushed and there were tire tracks on his clothing."

"Yeah, so?"

"And someone witnessed a blue pick-up truck crashed into a tree, on the same day as Karen's funeral. They said it backed up and the driver came out with a crowbar and did more damage to it."

Jason looked away, and his breathing became heavy. His heart began to race and the thoughts of the accident went through his head like flashes of memory hammering in his mind.

"Jason, did you hit that little boy?"

Alice's boyfriend had not said a word. His breathing was heavier and his eyes shifted back and forth very quickly. The silent treatment had given Alice the official response, that he did hit the little boy.

Alice could not believe it. Someone who she had fallen in love with and been dating since middle school had become the prime suspect of a murder. Her eyes began to fill up with tears as she approached her boyfriend and with her soft hands on his arms.

"Why did you do that?" Alice asked with a tear finally trickled down her left cheek.

"I said it was an accident." Jason responded nearly yelled. "I was too excited about the coach letting me trying out for the Carlton City's football team. And I ain't gonna let that slip away because some little kid wasn't properly supervised."

Alice's eyes began to water even more and her jaw slowly dropped from what she had just heard.

"You killed an innocent child and hid it's body just so you can play a stupid game?"

Jason slowly felt angry. He loved sports so religiously that for someone to call it stupid would be pure blasphemy to him. But having his girlfriend calling it stupid, felt like a pure insult to everything loved.

Alice's head went sideways. "I can't believe you!"

"What are you gonna do now?" Jason said.

"The right thing. I'm gonna call sheriff Barkley and clear this up."

Alice pulled out her cell phone and was about to phone the police station when Jason suddenly grabbed her wrist tightly and painfully.

"You will do no such thing." Jason sneered.

Alice was trying to pull off from her boyfriend's painful grasp.

"Let go of me!" she shouted. "You're hurting me!"

"I will not let you nor the police steal my dream away like that!"

"You murdered an innocent child, for fuck sakes!"

Jason grabbed her other wrist as Alice struggled to escape.

"I thought you loved me, Alice!" Jason said with wide, crazy eyes.

"Stop it! Your twisting my arm!"

"That's what you get for betraying me like that and call football stupid!"

"Hey!" A loud voice heard from a distance.

Alan appeared out of nowhere and flew a punch at Jason's nose. A faint *crunch* and Jason fell backwards, releasing his grip from Alice and hit the concrete floor with a bleeding nose.

"Get your fucking hands off my sister!"

Alan's attack didn't stop the hulking behemoth, it just made him madder. With years of sports training, he quickly got up raced toward his attacker and lunged him to the ground outside the garage. After the lunge, Jason threw a few punches into Alan's ribs but the young suspended cop had some self-defence training under his belt. He was able to press his left foot on Jason's six-pack and flung the sports jockey over him using all his strength on his left leg.

As Jason flew and crashed on his back, he looked back at Alan quickly getting up, waiting for the him make the next move. But Jason's head filled with rage and determination to keep his dream of becoming a football player. He didn't want to be thrown in jail, his opportunity was so close that he would do anything to achieve it, even it means covering up a murder.

Jason never hesitated to charge at Alan again. But this time, Alan dodge the hulking behemoth's charge and Jason nearly went over the back of the pick-up and into the bed. When took a g what was in there, he picked up a rusted crowbar, the same crowbar that he used to add extra damage to the truck after he rammed it into a tree.

He was about to take a swing at Alan when Alice jumped and grabbed his muscular hand from where crowbar would get its attacking power.

"Jason!" the crying girlfriend shouted. "Jason, stop it! Please!"

But her mad boyfriend ignored and swatted Alice with his other hand across her gentle, tear-eyed face. The impact of the hit made Alice flew and crashed into a pile of junk that was lying next to the pick-up truck.

"You motherfucker!" Alan shouted as he saw his sister just lying there with her hand on the side if her face, crying. "I'm gonna fucking..."

Alan was about to charge at Jason when the crowbar flew across his face. The impact had nearly broke his jaw and a couple of his teeth had escaped from his gums. He crashed to the ground barely conscious as Jason slowly walked up to his victim and drove his crowbar hard onto Alan's left arm which had let out a sharp *cracking* sound. Alan screamed in pain as he felt the bones in his arm snapped like a twig. He was about to do some more damage to him until he felt several shards of broken glass cutting through his scalp and the rest of the broken glass had passed by his face.

Jason looked back and it was Alice who had used a empty beer bottle on his head but the impact of it nearly made him dazed. His vision was blurring and saw a trickle of blood from his cut scalp going into one of his eyes.

"Jason, please!" Alice cried. "You've gone crazy!"

"I'm not crazy, Alice." Jason said "I'm a football player!"

And with that, the crowbar Jason had in his hand was pressing against Alice's throat, pushing against the driver's door of the pick-up.

"And I will do whatever it takes to become one, even if it means committing a murder....or two."

Alice suddenly became more afraid as the crowbar had pressed more onto her throat, cutting off from any scream she can possibly let out. The pressure of it was also cutting off her breathing, making chocking sounds and squeaks. She thought she was gonna die, killed by the hands of one person she had loved since they were kids. She could not give in to what he was doing to her, and thoughts of Jake Miller, alone in a jail, cell ran through her mind thinking that everything would have been different if she had been going out with him. She knew that he had a crush on her and even without showing or revealing it, keeping it away from the overprotective Jason Baker, Alice had small feelings for Jake as well.

There was a sudden chill, a deathly cold and tingling feeling ran up Jason's back. It felt unnatural and terrifying at the same time even for a sports jockey. He slowly looked behind him while still putting pressure on Alice's throat with the crowbar and noticed a giant black figure on the wall behind him. He assumed it was his shadow since one of the street lights had shined its light through a small window on the right side of the garage. He looked down at the figure's feet and realized they were connected to his own. His eyes went back up, and the figure suddenly emerged from the wall and gripped around his neck.

Alice was able to escaped from near death as the crowbar fell from her neck and she ran out of the garage toward her brother, still on the ground, groaning in pain. She looked back and saw the giant shadow that resembled Jason was pulling his counterpart toward the wall, toward the darkness it beheld. But even for what her boyfriend had done, for a hard-headed, self-centred, overprotective sports fan, Alice did not want him to go like that. Her conscious was telling her that and was also telling her that she should save him.

Alice ran up to Jason as he was getting pulled closer to the dark shadow. She grabbed onto one of his arms and attempted to pull, trying to free Jason from his own shadow. But while she was still pulling, she noticed that the shadow had formed into a face using the swirly, black pool that it was made out of. The face suddenly emerged and it appeared to be the face of a little boy, no younger than three years old. His face was covered in the black bile from the pool but half of his face was cracked like a broken vase.

It was him, the little boy that Jason had ran over with his pick-up truck. He let out a loud cry, louder than an average child of the same age. But the sound was unnatural and distorted, like someone had been playing with a sound board and mixed the cry with high and low pitches and different tempos.

Alan was able to turn toward the sound of the cry from where he laid, still grasping on his broken and swallowing some blood that was seeping out from his torn gums, from where some of his teeth had ripped through by Jason's crowbar. It noticed the shadowy figure that was pulling Jason toward it. He remembered seeing the same figure when he was visiting Dr. Cummings for questioning. He then noticed the face of the little boy, crying and screeching like a demonic child.

He wanted to get a good look on the child's face, just to be confirm it was the same one that Jason had killed. So he reached in his jacket for a small flashlight and beamed its light on the shadowy entity.

The child had screamed even louder, and the bright light from the flashlight was burning the entity. Little trickles of fire were shown on its surface, eating away the darkness and the swirly pool that made it. Jason was already halfway through and Alice was still pulling, crying and begging to have Jason back in her arms. But the burning effect was too much for the shadowy entity and dissolved completely.

Alice suddenly felt the force of the entity's strong pull vanished quickly and fell to the concrete floor against the driver side of the pick-up truck. As everything seemed to be back to normal, she felt as if there was something heavy, long and sturdy lying on her lap. As she looked down on her lap, she noticed it was really an arm. A muscular arm that she was familiar with. The same arm that had been around her body several times when she was in school and the same arm that she was using to try and save her boyfriend from what she may thought was certain death. When she realized who that arm had belonged to, she let out a loud and ear piercing scream.

Epilogue

The police station was quiet, quiet as the silence of death. The night gloomed in through the windows and dimmed the surrounding of the simple police officer guarding the jail cells from where Jake and Old Man Peterson were held. They both slept in their uncomfortable beds but Jake had a difficult time sleeping due to the loud snore that Old Man Peterson roared from the other side of the concrete wall.

Suddenly, the snoring had turned into little quirks choking and gargling. Then it finally stopped. Jake thought he had probably just died in his sleep but at least he was able to go back to sleep and rest peacefully. Though the plan of waking up the next morning would not have happen if Jake had not felt a cold breeze from within his jail cell.

The cold feeling was all to familiar to Jake. It was the same feeling he experienced when he was in his bedroom, before he saw his own shadow attacking him. From his bed he looked at the wall near his feet. The light from the hallway had casted a shadow over him and his bed but he could not see any abnormal movement except his own. It could possibly that the cold breeze may came from the small cracks in the wall which led to the exterior of the building, but it was too unnatural. It was too eerie and felt like the grim reaper had arrived in his soul and was ready to take him.

Jake turned his sleepy but startled eyes back and tried to close his eyes. But they flung wide opened for when he felt two large hands grasping his feet and began pulling toward the wall. He struggled and kicked as much as he could but the force of those shadowy hands were too strong for his kicks.

Jake's feet had gone through the wall, into the dark, swirly pool and his shoes were completely filled with the black, ice cold bile. He could barely feel the blood flowing through them and was already becoming numb. He tried to scream to the sleepy guard but he was too far off into dreamland to hear him. Even for Old Man Peterson who haven't heard all of the commotion that was going on, Jake assumed that the perverted old man had been taken away by his own shadow as well.

Holding on to the diagonal bar which kept the bed suspended in mid air, he held for dear life as his own shadow kept pulling. He looked back at the anomaly and saw a face that he had recognized from his childhood and recognized from previous experience with the dark entity. His mother, Olivia Miller emerged from his attacking shadow. Still covered in black slime, and eyes glowing yellow, she let out a huge cry which sounded distorted and multi-pitched. And just like before, she cried out the same words *'I'm sorry! I'm sorry!'* to her son who was about to meet her if the shadowy figure had pulled him in all the way. With his hands holding on tight to the diagonal bar, Old Man Peterson gone, and with his friends Alice and Alan beyond his reach, Jake shut his eyes tight and screamed.

To Be Continued...

www.ingramcontent.com/pod-product-compliance
Lightning Source LLC
Chambersburg PA
CBHW020152180626
46810CB00004B/1862